THE HOUSE
BY THE SEA

by

HILDA BODEN

COLLINS
LONDON AND GLASGOW

First printed in this edition 1965

Printed and Made in Great Britain by
Wm. Collins Sons and Co. Ltd.
London and Glasgow

CONTENTS

CHAPTER ONE

FARAWAY LANDING

PENNY leaned forward and stared through the wide window of the aeroplane.

"More water," she declared. "I think this is the sea. It's quite wide—do you think it's the English Channel?"

"Probably," said Geraldine. She did not move her fair head from the head-rest, but stared straight ahead of her, as she had done most of the time since they had left Nairobi airport the day before.

"It looks cold," decided Penny. "I liked the Mediterranean best. This looks like an angry sort of sea—I'd hate to be capsized in it."

"You're not likely to be capsized," said her sister coldly.

Penny sighed. Geraldine was not proving a pleasant travelling companion, and if it had not been for the pretty stewardess in the smart uniform, she would have been bored to tears.

"I do wish you would take an interest in something, Gerry," she complained. "Don't you think the flight is interesting? I do."

"And I do not," said Geraldine. "I didn't want to leave home and I don't want to live with strangers and I don't find it interesting at all."

"Uncle Ted and Auntie Clare aren't strangers. They're

Mother's brother. At least, Uncle Ted is. I liked the letter they wrote us. It sounded kind."

" They may be relatives, but they are strangers," said her sister obstinately.

Penny's voice wobbled. " I hope it will be nice, staying with them."

" Better than being at home in Kenya ? " asked Geraldine. Her own voice sounded clipped, because she was keeping a tight rein on her feelings.

" Kenya might not have been safe," said Penny gravely. " Mother told us so."

" Then she ought to have come here with us. If it isn't safe for us, it isn't safe for Mother and Daddy."

Penny bit her lip. She turned from the view and looked gravely at her elder sister. She had a tiny, elfin face and winged eyebrows that made her face usually look carefree, but at the moment it was stern.

" They're grown up," she said. " They can take care of themselves."

" I'm nearly fifteen," returned Geraldine. " I can take care of myself too. I've told you before how I feel about being bundled away from home and sent to people I've never met, just as if I were a paper parcel—or a kid of twelve."

This was meant to be an unkind dig at Penny, and Penny knew that it was, since she was only just twelve herself. Still, she was sorry for Geraldine, and worried about her because, ever since the journey to England and the unknown relatives had been arranged, Geraldine had been more than usually moody and sullen. She had sometimes been sullen before, but only for short intervals, when something had gone wrong at school, for example. This new phase of moodiness had lasted quite a long time, and Penny hoped it would end fairly soon. It would of course be marvellous if Geraldine could shake off the mood and brighten up and meet the new relations with a cheerful face. Penny tried to hit on something that might bring this about.

" I suppose England will be very interesting," she said diplomatically. " It's a very old country, isn't it? And I daresay you'll be able to do more exploring for antiquities, as you did in Kenya."

" Why? " asked Geraldine in the same cold tone of voice.

Again Penny bit her lip, but persisted.

" Well, because it *is* old. There'll be castles and things. You can explore them."

" The castles," stated Geraldine flatly, " are ancient monuments, or so I've read. They've been explored hundreds of times, and hundreds of books have been written about them. And the Stone Age camps have been explored, and all the Neolithic sites. It's only a little country, you know, and a great many people live in it."

" When we've finished with school," offered Penny, trying another and possibly more consoling idea, " you can go back to Kenya and finish exploring that site you found on our farm. You are sure to know a lot more about archæology by then."

Geraldine shrugged her shoulders, sat straighter in her seat, and gave a queer little snort. For one moment Penny thought her efforts had worked and that her sister was going to shake off the sullen mood, smile, and be pleasant again. But no. All Geraldine said was, " I suppose you are trying to make me forget that in a very few minutes we shall be meeting Uncle and Aunt and getting out of this aeroplane. Well, I shan't. I don't want to meet them and I don't want to live in England and I'd sooner stay in the plane the rest of my life, if I can't stay in Kenya. So there ! "

" You were jolly glad to get out of it at Khartoum," objected Penny. " I know I was. And wasn't it hot when we did get out ? "

" Naturally it was hot," agreed Geraldine. She added, scathingly, " Would you mind stopping this rather silly chatter ? My head is aching."

Penny's lips quivered. The pixie face looked woebegone.

" I don't think you're very nice," she told her sister. There was a hint of tears in her voice. " I don't feel very happy about coming here myself. Uncle Ted did sound kind in his letter, but perhaps they won't like us—he and Auntie Clare—when they see us. And I miss Mother and Daddy too, Gerry, and I think you're being rotten."

She gave a loud sniff and Geraldine, through the corner of her eye, saw the stewardess begin to move down the aisle towards them.

" Pull yourself together," she urged, under her breath. " For goodness' sake, don't start crying like a baby ! Here's my hanky. There. Blow your nose with it—hard. That's right. And stop making such a fuss."

The stewardess stopped by their double seat.

" Everything all right ? " she asked cheerfully.

Penny managed a weak little smile.

" Quite all right, thanks very much," she said.

" We'll be landing almost any time now," said the stewardess encouragingly. " It's been a tiring journey, hasn't it ? But there's England, see ?—coming up in front of you. See it ? See the white cliffs ? "

" It's *tiny*," exclaimed Penny, forgetting her troubles and watching a landscape of little houses and patchwork fields and blue threads that were rivers, unfold below.

" We're a long way up," the stewardess told her.

She walked away and Penny went on staring down.

" Everything's so close together," she said. " So many houses. There must be lots and lots of towns. Over Africa, it was all green and brown for miles and miles and hours and hours."

The stewardess turned at the end of the aisle. " Fasten your safety belts, please," she called.

" Fasten—is there something wrong ? " asked Penny, catching her breath.

" Don't be stupid," Geraldine told her. " It's just routine. You've fastened your safety belt before on landing and taking off. Here you are. I'll do yours for you. There."

Penny's voice was wobbly again.

" You think it will be all right, Gerry ? " she asked under her breath.

" I suppose you mean meeting the relatives," said Geraldine coolly. " I don't want to do it, and I don't suppose I shall enjoy it, but it has to be done because there's no way of avoiding it. And don't, for goodness' sake, let us down by starting to cry when you see them, or anything like that."

"I hope they're nice," said Penny.

Geraldine took no notice. She craned in front of her sister and stared down in her turn.

"We're braking. There. That must be the airport. Down there. All those buildings and all the other 'planes."

"I wonder where Uncle and Auntie are waiting for us?" said Penny.

Geraldine did not answer.

Down on the ground Ted Jones and his wife Clare were watching the big plane come in to land. He was a tall man with a cheerful face; his wife was fair and pretty with bright, eager eyes.

"Here they come," said Uncle Ted.

"I wonder if they'll like us?" said his wife.

"Sure to, if they've any sense," he told her, squeezing her hand. "There you are. Down they come. Perfect landing."

"A lot you know about that," said his wife, talking quickly because she was a little nervous at meeting these unknown nieces.

"And what about the R.A.F. and the war?" demanded Uncle Ted.

"Oh, that!" scoffed his wife. "That wasn't flying the same sized plane, was it?"

"Basically they work the same way," he told her gravely. The silvery 'plane with the red, white and blue stripes on its tail taxied along the landing strip until it slowed down enough to come to rest nearly opposite them. A small flag popped up at the stern, then a trolley was rolled up. The door in the side of the aeroplane opened and the portable ramp was placed against it.

" There they are," whispered Uncle Ted's wife, watching the passengers disembark. " That must be them— the two girls standing together. The tall one must be Geraldine. She's pretty, isn't she ? And the other looks a pet."

" She looks just like my sister used to when she was considerably younger than she is now," returned her husband, " and don't be misled by that piquant little face and those flyaway eyebrows. Sometimes, I admit, my sister was a pet. The rest of the time she was a plain rascal."

" And how about yourself ? " Aunt Clare demanded indignantly.

Uncle Ted kept a straight face.

" At times," he stated, " I may have faltered, but, on the whole, I did my best to set the girl a good example and bring her up to be a credit to me."

And then they stopped this interchange of small talk, which was, as they knew, a way of hiding the fact that they were both nervous, and went forward to greet their nieces.

" The Misses Wilds, I presume ? " said Uncle Ted gravely, making a sort of bow.

Penny knew at once that she was going to like him.

" Geraldine is Miss Wilds," she informed him, her small face lighting up. " I'm just Penny."

" So little money to travel so far ! " joked Uncle Ted.

" I'm not as little as all that," objected Penny. " I'm twelve."

Aunt Clare put in, " Don't tease her, Ted." To Penny she said, " We are so glad you are here. Was the journey a good one ? "

Penny slipped a hand in her new uncle's.

" Some of it was. It was interesting at first, but then it got boring. And it was hot in Khartoum ! Terribly hot ! I could hardly breathe. Coming to England was exciting, though. We loved looking down at all those tiny houses —just like a big map spread on the ground."

Aunt Clare and Geraldine had been looking at each other. The older woman spoke first. " You must be Gerry," she said, rather shyly.

Geraldine held out her hand. She shook her aunt's in the aloof manner that Penny found so irritating.

" I'm Geraldine Wilds. If you don't mind, I prefer to be called that. Shortening my name does make it sound so childish, don't you think ? "

" Gerry ! " put in Penny, horror-stricken. It certainly seemed as though her sister's mood was there to stay.

Uncle Ted regarded Geraldine thoughtfully. He gave Penny's hand a little squeeze, and then inquired, in an interested sort of voice, " Do I have to say Geraldine Wilds all the time ? It's rather a mouthful."

Gerry flushed. " Just Geraldine," she mumbled.

" Still a mouthful," he commented, " but have it your own way."

He stepped aside to talk to the stewardess, who was hovering near, and Penny turned on Gerry. " Nobody ever calls you Geraldine at home," she fumed. " You know they don't."

" Exactly," said Gerry, coolly and clearly, " but we are not at home, are we ? "

Uncle Ted caught the question as he turned back to them. He whistled softly under his breath before he went off to collect their luggage.

" I suppose the girl is feeling homesick," he told himself, as he walked away. " We'll put it down to that and hope it will pass off. If it does not—we've certainly acquired a problem child, Clare and I."

CHAPTER TWO

A NEW HOME AND A NEW SCHOOL

UNCLE Ted's house was a shock to both girls. It was squashed between two other houses so that there was just room for his small car to run into the garage set at the back of it. It had a narrow strip of garden that was mainly a square of green grass with darker green hedges on either side. Penny, staring out of the window of the room that Aunt Clare had led her to, saw tidy little gardens of about the same shape and size stretching to right and to left. Even in front of her were more tiny gardens, but these were partitioned off by a long brick wall instead of a hedge. She sighed. Her aunt heard the sigh.

" Is it very bad ? " she asked.

" It's different from Kenya," admitted Penny. Then, because she didn't want to be unfriendly, she added, " I don't suppose there's so much room, here."

Aunt Clare dropped a kiss on the tip-tilted nose.

" Space is at a premium," she assured her young niece solemnly. " I shouldn't be surprised if the estate agents don't start selling plots of England by the inch, instead of by the square foot. But there are parks, you know, and tennis courts at the end of the road."

" We have the National Park in Kenya," said Penny hopefully. " Daddy took us there once. Monkeys came to sit on the hood of the car, and a lion rubbed himself on the side of it. He wasn't a very big lion," she added truthfully, " but he was bigger than a cub. Daddy said he was quite big enough to be wandering about alone."

" I'm afraid our park isn't a bit like that," admitted Aunt Clare. " There are probably ducks and ducklings on the pond but monkeys are definitely out. And as for lions! We keep them in the zoo."

" How nice for the lions ! " put in Geraldine sarcastically. It was the first time she had spoken since she had seen the room she was to share with her sister.

Aunt Clare flushed a little. " They don't have to hunt for their food " she said. " That's something."

" I'm terribly hungry myself," Penny remarked simply.

Geraldine said " Penny ! " in a warning tone.

Penny grinned. " Oughtn't I to have said that ? But I *am* hungry, so there ! And I don't suppose Auntie minds my saying it."

Aunt Clare said that of course she didn't. She added that she was going to make tea at once, and vanished down the stairs.

Geraldine gazed at Penny gloomily.

" It's even more awful than I expected it to be," she pronounced.

At once Penny decided that the little room and the view of the gardens were not so bad as all that. " Why ? " she demanded.

Geraldine made a grandiose gesture.

" This. Just this. This poky little house instead of the ranch at home. Those stupid little gardens instead of fields and scrub. Everything."

"I think Auntie Clare tried to make it nice for us," said Penny, looking round the room. "There are flowers on the chest ... see? And there's a row of books on those shelves ... there are biscuits in this box ... and I'm sure the bedspreads are new, and they're very pretty."

"I don't believe there are any servants," said Geraldine, taking no notice of all this. "I haven't seen a soul except Uncle and Aunt."

"Perhaps you don't need servants in a little house," suggested Penny. "Perhaps you do all the work yourself."

Geraldine groaned.

"What? Cooking and bedmaking and dishes and all the rest of it? You're not going to tell me even you would like that, Penny Wilds."

"I don't suppose I would," replied Penny truthfully, "but if it's what Auntie does I'll do it too. At least, I'll help her if she'll let me."

Actually, the nearest to housework that the newcomers got that day was to two dishcloths, with which they dried the dishes that had been used at tea. Penny chattered and asked questions and found out about the cupboards and drawers that housed various things, but Geraldine maintained what she thought was a dignified silence. She remained aloof and dignified during the brief tour of London that followed, being not in the least impressed by the ancient grey walls of the Tower, nor the brown, turgid river that lapped those walls. She regarded the trappings of the Yeoman Warders with a distant air and refused to be enthusiastic about headsmen's axes or the crown jewels.

Uncle Ted led them home, ate supper with them, and saw them off to bed with thanksgiving. He mopped his forehead.

" This is a pretty kettle of fish," he said to his wife.

" Perhaps the journey didn't suit her," she replied diplomatically. They both knew that she was referring to Geraldine.

" How long did we undertake to have them ? " inquired Uncle Ted, as though he did not know.

His wife reminded him. " Until they leave school, Ted. You know this was the arrangement. Although, if your brother-in-law can make a good sale of his farm, he and your sister may be home within the year."

" I don't think he'll make a good sale," said Ted Jones gloomily. " I don't think he'll make a sale at all, not while there's all this political trouble out there. And he *has* to sell his farm to get some capital to live on here. I'm afraid we've got Geraldine for a long, long time."

" She'll improve," said his wife. " She's one of those people who are slow to settle down. And I think she's homesick, too. Anyway, she starts school to-morrow, and I'm sure that when she's with a crowd of girls of her own age, she'll feel better."

Uncle Ted cheered up.

" Ah, school," he said. " Good old school. I didn't particularly like mine while I was studying at it, but I'm sure school will be just the place for Geraldine."

" I hope," agreed his wife, more cautiously, " that Geraldine enjoys her school. It has a good reputation. I do hope she will."

Aunt Clare was, unfortunately, wrong.

To begin with, there was a small examination to decide which classes the girls would fit in best.

" You've been taught at home, I understand," said the headmistress. She looked at Geraldine with her head on one side, rather like a considering sparrow.

" We had visiting teachers," Gerry told her stiffly. " Besides, our mother was a teacher before she married. Naturally, she knew just what we ought to learn."

" Um," said the headmistress, not particularly caring for her new pupil. " Methods may have changed since your mother's time. I think you had better both work a short arithmetic paper for me, and then write a composition so that I can judge your grammar and spelling. What subject shall I suggest? I have it. Kenya, of course. That should do splendidly."

Geraldine bit her lip.

" It's rather a large subject. Couldn't we choose one for ourselves ? "

" Didn't you care for Kenya ? " inquired the headmistress, her grey head to one side again.

Geraldine did not answer, so Penny did it for her. She had decided that the headmistress was trying to be friendly, and she liked the perky way she held her head.

" We love Kenya," she stated flatly. " It's our home."

" So there must be much you can write for me about it," said the headmistress briefly. " I shall look forward to reading your compositions with interest." She rose from her desk and shepherded Penny to the far end of a long table. " Here is the arithmetic paper. I shall give you half an hour to do as many problems as you can. Here are pens. More paper. I think I can trust you both to work on your own, can't I? No helping Penny, Geraldine."

"Golly," said Penny, not answering the question because she was inspecting the arithmetic paper, "I don't think it would be much use if Gerry did help me. I don't think I can answer any of these sums, and I don't believe Gerry can either."

"Try," said the headmistress encouragingly, and left them to their labours.

The horrible result was that both girls were put into classes rather younger than their years.

"I'm sure you'll soon catch up," said the headmistress, still being encouraging. "At present, it would not be fair either to yourselves or to the rest of the class to put you in higher ones. Work hard and do your best, and I am sure you will soon be a great credit to your school."

She opened a door near the end of the long corridor and marched Penny inside. She introduced her to a tall and bright-faced class teacher and there Penny was left, feeling even smaller than usual and, most unexpectedly, shy. Being Penny, the shyness did not last, and before the bell rang for first break she had given a brief and impromptu lecture on the farm she had left behind only three days before, and decided that she was going to be great friends with the girl who sat at the next desk.

Geraldine was not so lucky.

The headmistress escorted her to the end of one corridor, down a shorter one, up a flight of stairs, and along a balcony that overlooked a large hall.

"We give the school play there," she said, gesturing to the stage at one end. "There are end-of-term dances,

too." Then she looked at Gerry closely. "I was surprised at your essay on Kenya," she observed. "I expected, as it had been your home for so long, that you would
have shown more interest in it."

"Kenya is my home," said Geraldine tightly. "It's
always been my home. I was born there. I didn't want
to come away."

"We all of us have to face up to things we don't like,
at one time or another," said the headmistress serenely.
"If we take our setbacks and disappointments in an
adult and sensible way, I think they often do good. That
way is character formed."

"I hate it here," muttered Geraldine sullenly. "I
knew I would, and it's even worse than I expected."

The headmistress paused. "Why?" she asked gently.

Geraldine hesitated, and then words came in a rush:

"Oh, in Kenya we had a big house. It was a lovely
house, with cool, big rooms. We had ponies. There were
lots of servants. Uncle Ted lives in a very small house
and Aunt Clare does all the work. . . . And I'd found a
place near the river, on the farm, back home, where I'm
sure there'd been an encampment long ago. Stone Age,
perhaps. I was digging there, and reading books about
archæology. Now somebody else will dig there, or it
will never be properly discovered." She stopped
abruptly.

"And these are all the reasons why you wish you were
back in Kenya?" prompted the headmistress.

"Mother and Daddy stayed behind," said Geraldine,
glaring at the floor. "It wouldn't have been so bad if
they had come to England as well."

"I'm sure they would have come if they could have done so," said the headmistress. "Things are unsettled there, now, aren't they? Your parents must have felt it wise to send you home. Because England is home, Geraldine. Don't forget that. It is your parents' home because they were born here, and it will be yours. That's one of the things about being British. Britons may be called to so many parts of the world, and it isn't always easy for them to go, or easy for their families. I know that, because my own father was a magistrate in India, and I left him and my mother when I was younger than you."

"But you didn't *have* to," muttered Geraldine. If she had known the ways of the school and the awe in which its headmistress was held, she might not have spoken so impertinently.

"Oh yes, I did. I needed to be educated, if I was to be much use in the world," returned the older woman. "If I had stayed in India, I would have had to go hundreds of miles from home to school. And the climate wasn't suitable for growing children. But I'm glad I have that background of growing up in another country. I've been back to India as a teacher since I grew up, and I look forward to visiting there again. I'm lucky to have so many friends, and so many ties, in two different parts of the world. Could you try to think that way?"

"I don't want to, thanks," said Geraldine rudely.

The headmistress bit her lip. She marched on down the balcony and Geraldine followed her. She opened a door. Gerry looked through it to a cluster of desks that seemed simply crowded with strange girls. She felt their

eyes boring into her as she walked across the room to the
dais where a middle-aged teacher was speaking in French.

" This is Geraldine Wilds," the headmistress introduced her. " She has come to us from Kenya, and may
be unused to some of the ways of this school. Geraldine,
this is your class teacher, Mademoiselle Minoret."

The middle-aged teacher addressed her in rapid
French, and Geraldine, whose French was almost non-
existent, listened in dismay. When the headmistress
turned away, saying she hoped Geraldine would be
happy in her class, she did not answer.

Within, though, she was fuming and hating. " I won't
ever like it. I won't be happy here," she told herself.
" I won't. I won't."

CHAPTER THREE

UNEXPECTED ARRANGEMENT

THE days went by; they grew into weeks. Penny settled down happily, although she still persisted in having a little cry every time a letter came from Kenya.

"I don't quite see why you have to cry," observed Geraldine, after she had watched her sister, curled up on her bed, sniffing and nibbling chocolate biscuits over the airmail letter.

"I don't *like* crying," explained Penny, with hurt dignity. "I don't even feel like crying. I think I cry a bit because it's so lovely to hear from Mother and Daddy and know they haven't forgotten us."

"Sometimes it seems as if you've forgotten *them*," said Geraldine, staring out of the window at the trim little garden.

"I never forget them," said Penny, with another sniff.

"It's Uncle Ted this and Auntie Clare that, and swinging on their arms and being tucked in at night just as if they were Mother and Father," said Geraldine morosely. "I don't see how you can do it. And when you do do it, I don't see why you have to cry over a letter from home."

"I like people who like me," stated Penny. "I like Uncle Ted and Auntie Clare, and I think they are very nice."

Geraldine turned away from the window.

" Of course. They are paid to be," she said casually.

Penny stared. " Paid to be nice ? "

" Paid for looking after us. Our clothes. Our food."

Penny got up from the bed. She began to smooth the coverlet, with her back turned to Geraldine. Then, in a queer, tight little voice, she said, " I do wish you'd stop being beastly, Gerry. You've been beastly for such a long while. Ever since we left Kenya, and that's simply ages ago. I don't think it's nice of you to be so horrid. You don't even try to be polite to Uncle Ted, and sometimes you're quite rude to Auntie Clare. Mother wouldn't like it. You know she wouldn't."

" Thanks for the lecture," said Geraldine, flushing crimson.

Penny wheeled round, crossed the room and flung her arms round her tall sister.

" It's only because I want us all to be happy, Gerry," she said. " We all used to be happy. I'm happy here, although of course I would like it better still if Mother and Daddy were with us. And they will come some day, and they won't like it if we're not friends with Auntie and Uncle."

Geraldine disengaged herself. She turned to the little dressing-table and began to brush her hair.

" I sincerely trust," she remarked, " that I shall not have to stay in this house until Mother and Father come home. That might mean years, and I don't think I could bear it."

Penny hesitated, but there is not much that can be done with a sister who is brushing her long hair over her face, so she shrugged her shoulders and ran downstairs whistling cheerfully.

"You sound happy," remarked Aunt Clare, who was busy slicing bread in the kitchen.

"I am," Penny agreed. "It's the end of the school week. No more school till Monday. I'm usually happy, but specially so when there isn't going to be school to-morrow."

"I thought you liked your school," said her aunt.

Penny nodded vigorously. "I do, oh! I do. I like the painting lessons and gym and the games and most of the girls, but then, there's all that work. All that home-work. I don't think I like homework very much."

"You'll soon catch up with the rest of the class," Aunt Clare comforted her. "Once you've caught up, you'll find everything much easier."

"And there'll be holidays soon," said Penny thought-fully, accepting the slice of thickly buttered bread that was passed to her. She ate half the bread, and then added, "What shall we do for our holiday? Most of the girls in my class seem to be going to the seaside. Shall we go too? I've never seen the sea except from that aeroplane."

Neither of them had noticed that Geraldine had come downstairs and was standing at the door, so they both jumped when she said sarcastically, "I imagine we shall stay here in this delightful house, with an occasional con-ducted tour of the City of London as a holiday treat."

Aunt Clare flushed rosily, bit her lip, and bent her head.

Penny jumped from the table.

"Geraldine," she began, and choked on a crumb.

Aunt Clare tried to be composed, although her fingers trembled as she went on slicing the bread. " Where would you like to spend your holiday, Gerry ? Have you any suggestions ? "

Geraldine tossed her head. She replied, in a mildly contemptuous voice, " Does it really matter what I would like ? I would like to be addressed by my full name, for instance, and not that ridiculous abbreviation, yet my feelings are not taken into account."

Aunt Clare bit her lip even more tightly. The knife slipped and a long red line appeared across her hand. Blood began to spurt from it.

Two things happened at once. Penny sprang across the room and caught her aunt's arm ; and Uncle Ted's voice, speaking with unknown sternness, said from the hallway outside, " Go straight to your room, Geraldine, and stay there. I will attend to you later."

He strode across to his wife and loosened Penny's hands.

" Run away," he told her. " Leave this to me. Go out in the garden and play." He caught a glimpse of her white face. " I'm not angry with you, dear," he added, " but I can deal with this better by myself."

Penny obediently left the kitchen and closed the door behind her. Geraldine was at the foot of the stairs, standing there, hands clenched, eyes very bright.

" He ordered me out of the way as if I were a house-boy," she said.

" If I were you," counselled Penny, marching past her sister, " I'd do what he said. I think Uncle Ted is really angry."

She went out into the garden and found the lawn mower and began to mow the little green lawn. Geraldine walked slowly up to her room. She stood by the window, watching Penny pushing the lawn mower, and tried to justify herself.

" I can't make myself like being here, if I don't like it," she said to herself. " I didn't ask to come here and I didn't want to come. And Uncle Ted has no business to talk to me like that—as if I were a child. Aunt Clare cut her hand, but it wasn't my fault. If she's so clumsy that she can't hold a knife straight, I don't think it's anything to do with me."

Downstairs, Uncle Ted would not have agreed with this.

He had bathed the wound and was holding a compress against it. His wife's head was on his shoulder. She was sobbing, deep heavy sobs.

The blood began to stop oozing from the sharp cut, but the sobs did not stop. Uncle Ted said gently, " Come now, Clare. It isn't really as bad as that. I'll bandage it soon, and Penny and I will do all the washing up until it's healed, so's to give it a chance."

" It isn't Penny," sobbed Aunt Clare. " It's the other one."

" Gerry ? "

There were confused noises from his shoulder that he took to mean agreement.

" But a schoolgirl can't upset you like this," he said, looking very worried.

His wife sniffed, looked up at him out of wet, woebegone eyes, and returned, " You don't know what it's

like. I didn't mean to tell you. She's never very polite
or pleasant to you, but you don't see so much of her.
She's horrid to me. She tries to make me feel small, and
often succeeds. That's how I happened to cut myself. I
was trembling because I was trying to keep control of
myself and not fly out at her."

"Letting go at her might do some good," suggested
Uncle Ted mildly. "Also an occasional flip on the ear
might be in order."

He reached for his handkerchief and began to wipe
his wife's face.

"She's not my child," said Aunt Clare, in a low voice.
"I don't think I've any right to correct her like that."

"I don't know what my sister and brother-in-law have
been doing to let the child grow up like this," said Uncle
Ted. He went across to a cupboard, fetched a neat roll
of bandage, and began to wind it around the injured hand.
"There you are. Doesn't hurt so much now, does it?
How's that?"

"Lovely," sighed his wife. She hesitated, and then
added, "I oughtn't to have said so much about a child
who can't answer back, Ted. Forget it."

"That's all very well," he told her. "I was quite
prepared to make a home for my nieces, in this emergency, but not at the expense of my wife. We have to
think what can be done."

"There isn't anything that can be done, Ted. I'll have
to pull myself together and stand up to Geraldine more.
There! I said Geraldine. She'd be pleased to hear
that."

"I doubt if she would," said Uncle Ted dryly. "I

think she only tries to insist on it to be annoying." He began to walk about the room.

" If we could send them somewhere for the holidays," suggested Aunt Clare. " Penny was talking about holidays just before you came in. Perhaps we could find a nice farmhouse somewhere where they would be safe and cared for without us going too."

Uncle Ted thrust his hands deep in his pockets.

" It's an idea, but I imagine we have waited rather long to arrange anything like that. It's July now, and you know how holiday accommodations get booked up. I'll make inquiries, but I should think we're too late to find anything really good. The good places will have been booked months ago."

" Well, it was an idea," said Aunt Clare.

Her husband suddenly slapped his leg and gave a shout of laughter.

" What is it now ? " inquired his wife cautiously.

" Your Aunt Pru," said Uncle Ted.

His wife stared at him.

" Lovely house. By the sea. Bathing, boating, all the holiday attractions. Just the place for my sister's girls."

" And how about Aunt Pru ? " demanded his wife.

" Aunt Pru," stated Uncle Ted, " can look after herself. I've never met a woman more capable of looking after herself. If she'll have the girls, she'll take them in her stride. If Gerry tries any Geraldine-ing, she'll suffer from wholesome neglect. Now I come to think of it, Aunt Pru is probably just made for Geraldine."

" She wouldn't have them," said his wife.

She turned to the table again and reached for the bread and butter, but he took them away from her.

" Leave this to me. I'll finish getting tea. If I can't cope, I'll yell for Penny and she'll give me a hand. And to-night, I'm going to phone your Aunt Pru and explain matters. We don't know whether she'll say No or not, until we give her the chance."

They gave her the chance, and Miss Prudence Chart— Aunt Pru—said "Yes."

CHAPTER FOUR

UNKNOWN WALES

"GOING to Wales for our holiday?" repeated Penny. She looked at Uncle Ted worriedly. "Are you coming too?"

"Do you want me to?"

Penny nodded. Uncle Ted laughed. "Nice child," he told her. "In some ways, I almost wish I was. But not this time. You're going by yourselves."

Penny leaned against him. "I do wish you were coming."

"You'll like Aunt Pru," promised Uncle Ted. "You'll like her house, too. It's lots bigger than this one, and there are fields and woods belonging to it that go right down to the sea."

"I hope Aunt Pru will like me," said Penny wistfully.

"I'll send a special message with you, to tell her to be sure she does," he promised gravely.

"That's a joke," said Penny, "but I know what I'll do. I'll knit this new aunt some bed-socks. I started knitting some bed-socks for you, before we came here, but somehow, they never got finished. The wool's in my travelling case, I think, and an unfinished sock." She turned to the other person in the room. "Would Aunt Pru like bed-socks, Auntie Clare?"

"She might," said Aunt Clare cautiously.

"I suppose she's pretty old, as she's your aunt," said Penny serenely. "I should think her old legs would like bed-socks. I'll find that wool when I go to bed and start knitting again. Most people like being given presents, so, if I start with a present, perhaps she'll like me."

"Just go on being pleasant and willing, Penny, and people will go on liking you without presents," advised Uncle Ted.

There was so much to do! Clothes, which included shorts and swimsuits, had to be discussed, and afterwards bought, and what with that, and end-of-term celebrations, and examinations—which were quite horrible—and report cards that could have been, on the whole, somewhat worse, the remaining days of July simply flashed by.

Geraldine did not take much part in the holiday preparations. She had been wary of her uncle ever since he had ordered her to her room on that unfortunate afternoon. Aunt Clare talked to her less than she had ever done. Gerry told herself she was glad to be left alone, but sometimes she envied Penny, trying on holiday clothes after a shopping expedition and squealing excitedly as she postured before the mirror.

Geraldine had declined both shorts and swimsuit, announcing, grimly, that she was devoting her holiday to studying French, and therefore would have no need of them.

"How nice for you!" commented Uncle Ted, and Geraldine did not reply.

Then, quite suddenly, it seemed, school was over for the term, satchels were carried back without homework in them, their suitcases were packed again, and they were ready for the long journey across England that would end very late at night in Wales. Uncle Ted and Aunt Clare saw them off at the big station, Penny with hugs and kisses, and Gerry with injunctions to have a good time. The girls settled down for the trip. At first the sun shone brightly over the fields so that it was almost too hot in the railway carriage, and then its rays grew longer and the air chillier, until darkness closed around the train that snaked its way through an unseen country-side like an enormous glowworm.

The train began to slow down again, and Penny, who had been dozing uncomfortably in her corner of the carriage, rubbed a circle clear from mist on the window-pane and peered out.

" I think we're coming to another station," she said hopefully. " I can see lights. I hope we are, because this must be the end of our journey. I'm quite stiff with sitting still."

" It won't be exactly the end of our journey," said Geraldine, taking a comb out of her hold-all and begin-ning to smooth her hair. " Don't you realise that we still have ten miles to go when we leave this train ? I hope there's a taxi, but you never can tell. We may be met by a pony and trap, as this place is so far from civilisation. That would take us at least another two hours."

" It does seem terribly late for an old lady to come to meet us," agreed Penny. " I hope she doesn't have to drive a pony and trap."

" Even if she meets us with one, she is hardly likely to drive it herself," said Geraldine, in her most superior manner.

Penny took a deep breath. She started to say, as she had been meaning to say ever since they got in the train, how much she hoped that her sister would like Aunt Prudence Chart, and other things like that. It had not been easy to start saying them to an older sister, and they never did get said, as it happened, because the train drew up at a long, empty platform with a jerk.

Penny stood up and let down the window. She leaned out.

" I suppose Aunt Pru is sitting down somewhere waiting for us," she remarked. " Poor old lady, I hope she isn't very tired. And I never did finish that bed-sock for her. Still, I knitted a nice big piece of leg, and I'll show it to her so's she'll know I have been thinking of her. If it rains a lot and there's nothing much to do, I might finish both of them while I'm in Wales."

Geraldine took down a suitcase from the rack.

" Isn't there anybody on the platform ? " she demanded.

" Just two men, a long way down it," said Penny.

" If you opened the door and jumped out," suggested Geraldine, struggling with the other suitcase, " you might attract their attention and we might get help with these. They're heavy."

" Sorry," said Penny contritely. She opened the door and jumped down to the platform and Geraldine handed the cases to her. The two people farther down the station turned and began to walk towards them, and one of them waved a hand.

" That can't be Aunt Pru, can it ? " said Penny, in a

half-whisper. " It can't. I mean, it *is* a woman, but she's wearing slacks ! "

" I hardly think it can be Aunt Prudence," agreed Geraldine, taking in the tall, thin woman who was walking towards them, in her casual outfit of corduroy trousers and duffel coat.

" She's pretty old," said Penny. " She's got grey hair, but she doesn't walk as if she was old."

" I imagine that a friend has been asked to meet us," said Geraldine, but the stranger strode right up to them, held out a firm brown hand, and smiled.

" This is Gerry and Penny Wilds, isn't it ? You must be, because you are the only passengers to get off the train. I'm Prudence Chart. How did the journey go ? The train's late, of course."

" Now, Miss Chart," said the man who accompanied her and who wore a blue uniform and a porter's cap, " that's unfair. Train's on time, to-night."

Miss Chart consulted her watch.

" Ten minutes late," she said briskly. " I have known it to be slow by half an hour. Sometimes I wonder you don't mislay your trains, Evan. One day one of them will get lost in the mountains and never be heard of for years, only nobody at this station will realise that, and when it finally does turn up, you'll signal it in as if nothing was wrong."

" Look you now, Miss Chart," protested the porter. " Your train from the north, last time you came in, was a little late, I grant you. And a long time ago that was."

" Just under the hour late," said Miss Chart firmly, " and it was only a month ago."

The porter pushed his cap to the back of his head.

" Try to think of our passengers, we do," he protested again. " You wouldn't like it yourself, Miss Chart, if we knew you were leaving by a particular train and you were a little bit late and the train didn't wait for you ? Would you, now ? Well, then. If there are passengers a bit late all along the line . . . there you have it ! "

" I don't know what the railway authorities would say about it, but there we have it," agreed Aunt Pru gravely. " And I agree that, on the whole, it's a pleasant, neigh- bourly way to run a railway, until it results in losing a connection farther down the line. I'm only pulling your leg, Evan."

Penny had listened to all this, quite entranced, and now she put in, without thinking, " I thought you were."

" Miss Chart is always pulling somebody's leg," said the porter. " Wait you until she gets going on yours."

Miss Chart did not comment. She looked at the suit- cases. " Any more luggage ? " she demanded.

" A small trunk, in the guard's van," said Geraldine. She was not sure that she was going to like this strange new aunt. Miss Chart was not at all like anybody she had imagined as Aunt Clare's own aunt, and she could not size her up.

The trunk and the two suitcases were loaded on a trolley by the porter and the train drew away from the station.

" Put them in the back of the van, Evan," directed Miss Chart. " There's a sack of corn and another of potatoes that Tommy Owen asked me to pick up for him, but you can push those together. Take care of the big box, though. There are records in that, and I wouldn't want them damaged."

" Music records ? " asked the porter hopefully.

Miss Chart nodded. " Bach. I don't think we have them in the village. We'll have a musical evening and you must all come and listen to them, sometime."

Evan pushed the trolley briskly in front of them, and they followed him over the level crossing, on to the far platform, and outside the station. The moon was shining brightly, lighting their way across the rails. Outside the station it outlined a background of peaked mountains and massed trees. There was a sound of running water.

" Is there a river ? " asked Penny.

" Only a brook," said Miss Chart. " There's always water running somewhere in Wales, even if it isn't raining, which it does quite a lot. It's having the mountains so near, you see."

The van was waiting round the corner. It was quite big, and painted a cheerful scarlet.

" Are we going in that ? " demanded Geraldine.

Miss Chart nodded.

" It's much more useful to me than an ordinary car would be. And the front bench seat is quite wide. I'm sure we can all fit on it. Unless, that is, either of you prefers to travel in the rear with two sacks and a wooden box."

Penny giggled. " They sound bumpy," she said, and climbed into the front seat and settled close to the driver. Miss Chart felt warm and kind. Penny thought she was going to like her a lot.

" It's only ten miles to Yr Hafan," said this strange

aunt, driving efficiently away from the little station. " It won't be quite as quick as it sounds because they are ten twisting and hilly miles. But we shall be home before midnight. I suppose you are longing for bed."

" I was," admitted Penny, staring through the windshield at the lane that was revealed by the sweeping brightness of the headlights. It was only just wide enough to take the van, and she thought there was grass growing down the middle of it. On either side of the lane she thought there were steep banks, but they were so trailing with greenery it was difficult to tell. Beyond the banks the land sloped up steeply, and beyond that, where the moon was riding serenely above them, she was sure there were the jumbled peaks of mountains. She was glad she was squashed so close to the driver. By herself, in this unknown country, she might have felt afraid.

" I left some soup on the stove," said Miss Chart, rounding a bend so sharp that the lane bent back on itself. " I can also make omelettes, if you are terribly hungry."

" I *am* hungry," said Penny happily, liking her new aunt more than ever. " I'm so hungry I feel hollow inside."

" Good," said Miss Chart. " I like people to enjoy their food. And I hope you are not fussy about what you eat. I hate folk who fuss."

" I eat anything," said Penelope, even more happily, " though I do prefer not to eat soggy vegetables if I can help it."

" My vegetables," stated Aunt Pru, " never sog. I

grow them in the garden, where the slugs try to eat them before I can. They are too precious to waste."

"You are fond of cooking?" asked Geraldine, feeling that it was time she made an effort to join in the conversation.

"I like to cook," said Miss Chart. "I like many things. The older I grow the more I find what fun it is to spread one's likings widely. What are your particular affections, Gerry? It *is* Gerry, isn't it? I know you are the older sister."

"Actually, it's Geraldine," said the owner of that name, in the sort of voice that her sister dreaded hearing. "I do feel that an abbreviation is so childish. Penny, of course, is really Penelope, but I hope she will grow out of that, soon."

"Shall you, Penny?" inquired Miss Chart.

"I hope not," said Penny, very cross with Geraldine, and hoping that she was not going to create the unpleasant atmosphere with the new aunt that she had achieved with the old. But the new aunt was made of sterner stuff than Aunt Clare, who would have blushed faintly, and been hurt.

"Actually," said Miss Chart, shifting gears as the van began to labour up a hill so steep it seemed to point to the moon itself, "actually I'm not your aunt, of course. As your aunt-in-law's aunt, we are not even related at all. So, if you would prefer to call me by my surname—with Miss in front of it—I shan't be in the least put out. Suit yourself, Geraldine."

Penny gave Gerry's ankle a little kick that tried to tell her to be sensible and laugh this off and agree to be known by her nickname after all. Geraldine took no notice of the kick, save to twist her leg safely out of the way.

" Yes, Miss Chart," she said meekly.

Miss Chart accepted this, without comment. She slowed down, and negotiated a downward twisting slope carefully. The headlights shone against two heavy stone pillars with a gate set open between them. Between the pillars a weedy drive led to a square, solidly built stone house. It looked sensible and comfortable and safe.

Miss Chart stopped before the stout front door.

" Home," she said, opening the driver's door. " Out you go. Welcome to Yr Hafan."

CHAPTER FIVE

BREAKFAST IN BED

PENELOPE fell asleep thinking she heard the sound of water, and when she woke up again she was sure of it. There was a small, watery noise as though something was being upset, quite close at hand ; there was the swift rushing noise that the brook near the station had made the night before ; and there was a distant, gentle roar that still had the sound of water in it.

Across her pillow sunlight was falling in a bright band of light, so that she blinked when she opened her eyes.

Somebody said, " *Dash!* " with great emphasis.

Penny quite woke up, to see that her new aunt was standing by the bed carrying a laden tray. She dumped it on the little chest beside the bed, and said cheerfully, " This morning you are being spoiled. It won't go on, because I don't believe in spoiling people, but you did look so very tired last night. Here's breakfast. I'm terribly sorry, but I jerked the milk jug and it's splashed the tray. Before that, it all did look rather nice."

Penny sat up and regarded the breakfast tray with satisfaction. It seemed to hold something of everything. " It looks like a gorgeous breakfast," she said.

Aunt Pru mopped up the spilt milk with her hanky.

" Between you and me, Penny," she said solemnly,

" I'm not a very good housekeeper. I like cooking, but I know I'm careless, and quite often I forget things."

" I forget things, too," admitted Penny. " Uncle Ted says not to worry if I've been born that way, because other things can make up for it."

Aunt Pru laughed.

" What a consoling thought! I only hope that I have sufficient good points to make up for my failings. And I hope there's something you like on that tray. As I didn't know your tastes, I put on something of everything I like myself. There's porridge and toast and home-made marmalade and butter from the farm and one of Mrs. Morgan's biggest brown eggs and milk to drink. I would have offered bacon as well, but I forgot to buy any yesterday, and it will be two more days before the travelling shop calls again."

"I couldn't possibly have managed bacon," said Penny, lifting the tray across her knees. " This is wonderful, and thank you very much. I've never had breakfast in bed before. May I start?"

" Do," urged Miss Chart heartily. She walked over to the window and pulled the curtain wide open. Sunshine flooded the room. " Do you mind if I smoke?"

Delighted at being treated as an adult, Penny said that she did not, and began to eat the porridge.

" I think I'd better explain how this household works," said Miss Chart, blowing a little blue smoke ring that drifted away in the sunshine motes. " You see, I'm a working woman. I'm used to having my time to myself. So, although I hope I don't sound unkind, I'll expect you and your sister to amuse yourselves. If the weather is good, there is boating and bathing, and I'll join you in those. Otherwise, there is the beach and the woods and the hills and you will have to make the best of them."

" It sounds like a lot to make the best of," said Penny, finishing the porridge and taking the top off the egg. " I'm sure I'll be able to do it."

" Well, that's up to you," said Aunt Pru. She blew a second smoke ring, regarded it, and went on. " Then there's the house routine. Dilys Owen comes in daily and cleans for me, so that's no trouble. We have to be a little careful about electricity, because we make our own and it isn't as simple as having it supplied by a main power house. Can you hear the motor purring ? That's our source of power. It's quite good, but before you turn on a light, or the stove—if you feel like cooking— make sure a lamp is switched on first. The engine doesn't like a large apparatus switched on suddenly. That's all there is to remember about that, because Tommy Owen, Dilys's husband, who lives with her in the cottage down our own lane, looks after it. Just as well, because I'm hopeless at mechanics myself, and I'd surely forget to put oil in the machine when it wanted it."

Penny made mental notes of these things.

Aunt Pru went on : " Then, we're miles away from any shops as perhaps you've guessed. There's a little town with a few shops near the station where I picked you up last night, but we rely mainly on the travelling shops that drive round the district. The grocer's shop will call in two days' time. The butcher's calls to-night. We catch our own fish. The baker's comes every other day, and it carries important things like chocolate and biscuits as well as cake and bread. The postman, Davies Post, comes every morning, except Sunday, about eleven. Davies Post is very helpful. He will take letters and parcels and provide stamps for them if we run short ourselves. I think that's the lot."

" I'll try to remember it all," promised Penny, starting on the last slice of toast. " I'm specially glad you told me about the stamps, because I didn't bring any air-mail postage with me, and I always write to Mother and Daddy every week. Do you think the postman will have an air-mail stamp ? "

" If he hasn't," said Miss Chart, " he will bring one for you to-morrow, if you ask him nicely. Davies Post likes his services to be appreciated."

" Why do you say Davies Post ? " asked Penelope, before she ate the last scrap of toast.

" You've only to look in our local telephone book to know that, my child. There are seven whole pages devoted to subscribers with the name of Davies ! Wales hasn't nearly so many surnames as England has. There are lots of Davieses and Owenses and Morgans and Griffiths and Joneses. The easiest way to distinguish one from another is to tack on an occupation or a place to the name, like Davies Post, the mail man, or Morgan, Pentre, our nearest farm and where we get our milk."

" You'd be Chart, Yr Hafan ? " suggested Penelope.

" I would," agreed her aunt, " if there were many Charts. As it is, I seem to be unique in the area."

Penny parked the empty tray carefully on the chest and slipped out of bed. She went to stand beside her aunt. Looking out of the window she saw an entrancing view of a little shining brook running swiftly through a thin strip of woodland. Behind the house, hills rose to the mountainous skyline, but the brook ran down through a narrow valley, and at the end of the valley dark cliffs penned in a pool of blue.

" Like it ? " asked Miss Chart, following Penny's gaze.

Penny drew a deep breath.

" It's wonderful. It's just wonderful to stand here and look at it. Is that the sea ? May I go down to it ? I've never been near the sea."

" You may," said Aunt Pru, " with the proviso that you don't try to swim unless I'm there. That is, until I'm sure of your swimming."

" I can't swim," said Penny truthfully, " but I'm going to learn." She leaned over the window sill and breathed deeply of the fresh salty air. " What does Gerry think of it ? "

" Haven't asked her," said Miss Chart briefly.

Penny withdrew her head. She looked just the least little bit worried. " Hasn't Gerry had her breakfast in bed ? "

Miss Chart shook her head calmly. " I wouldn't dream of intruding on her. There'll be breakfast downstairs for her when she wakes up."

Penny hesitated. She rubbed one bare toe on the carpet. She thought hard. She seemed to have done such a lot of explaining about Gerry since they had left Kenya, and none of it had done much good. She had tried to explain to Uncle Ted and to Aunt Clare, and she had tried to talk to Geraldine herself. She was not sure that more explanations were worth while. Then, because Miss Chart was kind and sensible, in spite of her abrupt manner and outright statements, she tried once more.

" Gerry hasn't been quite like herself since we left home. I think going away worried her a lot."

" It didn't worry you ? " demanded Miss Chart.

" Oh, it did ! " exclaimed Penny indignantly. " It worried me a great deal, but I knew Mother and Daddy wouldn't have sent us away unless they simply had to. We . . . we're awfully fond of one another," she ended lamely, and her voice wobbled.

Aunt Pru heard the wobble in the voice.

" What fun you'll all have telling one another about your experiences, when they come home too."

Penny looked at her solemnly.

" That's a nice way to think about it. I'll try to see it that way."

" Perhaps Geraldine might try to think that way," said Miss Chart dryly.

" Gerry had so much more to leave, I suppose," said Penny. " I just had Mother and Daddy, and that was bad enough, but she had her pony and her excavation, and——"

" What excavation ? " demanded Miss Chart.

Penny looked surprised at this interest.

" Oh, I only saw it once. It wasn't very interesting. Just a cave that went quite a long way into the hillside and had some squiggles drawn on one of the walls. Gerry thought it was very old and started digging the floor up."

Miss Chart looked vexed.

"I hope she didn't do any damage."

"There really wasn't anything to damage," Penny assured her. "And Gerry has read lots of books about how to excavate. Lots and lots. The library in Nairobi lent them to her."

"I hope she digested their substance properly," said Miss Chart.

Penny lost interest in the question of Geraldine's excavation. She had remembered something else and made a dive for her suitcase.

"I'm so glad I thought of this," she said, making hay of the clothes packed inside it, while she searched for something. "Here it is. I made it for you when I knew we were coming here. I thought you'd be old and it would be nice for your feet at night."

"Why did you think I'd be old?" asked Miss Chart, watching a peculiar piece of knitting being dragged from the suitcase.

"Well, Aunt Clare is getting old, isn't she? And you're *her* aunt." Penny suddenly realised she might be treading on dangerous ground, and stopped short. "Anyhow, now that I've met you, I know that you're not old at all," she finished.

"I'm glad of that," agreed Miss Chart gravely. She accepted the knitting, complete with needles and a ball of wool. She held it up in front of her. "I never was good at knitting," she added, "and I don't seem able to make out what this is, and why it should be useful for cold feet."

"It's a pair of bed-socks," explained Penny. "At

least, it's half a pair, or it will be, when I've finished it. I'll finish it while I'm here. I do want to make you a present."

She, also, stared at the bed-sock. There seemed a great deal of knitting to be done before even that one was finished. She sighed.

Aunt Pru heard the sigh. She smiled, laid down the knitting, and said, " Do you mind if I look a gift horse in the mouth, Penny ? I know it's a shocking thing to do, but facts are facts. And one fact is that I seldom suffer from cold feet, and if I do, I have an electric blanket to switch on. And the other is that if you cast off the stitches on those needles and sewed one end together, there'd be a marvellous oven glove, and I'd simply love an oven glove."

Penny breathed deeply and thankfully. " That's a lovely idea."

Aunt Pru picked up the tray. " I'll take this down to the kitchen. Perhaps you'd see if Geraldine means to wake up to-day, when you're dressed."

" May I wear shorts ? " asked Penny.

" They are most suitable," agreed Aunt Pru. " I often wear them myself, particularly in the boat."

And she vanished through the door.

Penny dressed quickly and tapped on her sister's door. Geraldine, in a sleepy voice, told her to come in.

" Golly," said Penny, entering the darkened room, " aren't you awake yet ? I'll draw the curtains, shall I ? That's better. The sun's shining, and it's a lovely day. And oh, Gerry, this is a lovely place. There's the sea, and there's a boat."

Geraldine rolled over crossly. "Is there breakfast?" she demanded.

"I've had mine," said Penny incautiously. "I had it in bed, on a tray. Aunt Pru says yours will be downstairs when you want it."

Geraldine grunted.

"Aunt Pru said she thought I looked tired last night," added Penny, trying to explain away the breakfast-in-bed.

"I didn't want a breakfast tray," said Gerry. Her face put on its closed, brooding look.

"You'll like it here," Penny assured her, hoping that she was speaking the truth.

"That remains to be seen," returned Geraldine. She scrambled out of bed. "Run along, and as soon as I'm dressed I'll come downstairs."

Penny went away, along the landing, down the wide, polished stairs, through a cool hall and towards voices she could hear. They came from a big, sunny kitchen.

Gerry stared bitterly out of her window. She would have to make the best of it again. Nobody wanted her. Not Mother, nor Father, nor the uncle and aunt in London. And now not the new Aunt Pru.

CHAPTER SIX

TO FETCH THE MILK

PENNY ran down to the kitchen. It was quite easy to find because she could hear conversation coming from it, and one of the voices was Aunt Pru's.

The kitchen was cool, flagged with smooth slabs of stone. There was a modern stove set in a wide alcove that had once been an ingle-nook. Against the opposite wall was a tall Welsh dresser with many shelves full of gay jugs and plates. An enormous table stood in the centre of the flagged floor. One end of it was set for a meal, and a short, stout woman was polishing silver at the other.

" This is Dilys Owen," said Miss Chart, " and here is my visitor, Dilys. This is Penny."

The plump woman smiled ; her dark eyes twinkled in her brown face. " Look you," she said, " my morning it is for cleaning the silver. Dirty my hands are with the polish, so I will not shake with you, but bid you *croeso.*"

" Thank you very much," said Penny. She hesitated, and then added, " Please, what does it mean ? "

Miss Chart blew a smoke ring. " Dilys," she observed, " speaks Welsh. *Croeso* means Welcome. If you want to learn the language, you must coax Dilys to teach you."

Penny went over to the silver-cleaning end of the table and leaned on it excitedly. " Would you ? Would you really? I'd love to learn Welsh. I didn't know it was a separate language from English until I came to England. It must be very exciting to have a special language of your own. Secret, and special."

Mrs. Owen seemed pleased. " An older language than the English is our Welsh tongue. It will be a pleasure to teach you a little of it, but, look you, it is not a speech that can be learned in one day."

She rubbed a silver salver vigorously, and Penny nodded, entranced.

" To begin with," said Mrs. Owen, " you shall wish me *Boreu da*, and that will be good morning."

Penny repeated the strange words carefully.

" Not too bad," commented Dilys. " Maybe you have the tongue for the Welsh. But there is no time for more, because Miss Chart will be wanting you to fetch the milk—and here is the other young lady come down for her breakfast."

Geraldine was indeed standing in the doorway.

Miss Chart sketched a casual gesture with her cigarette. " My other visitor, Miss Geraldine Wilds."

The shrewd brown eyes regarded Geraldine coldly. " Indeed, and so it must be," Dilys commented.

Geraldine flushed.

Miss Chart rose from her chair, tossed her cigarette stub into the fire, and took up an enamel can with a lid.

" I do want the milk," she said to Penny. " I was going to put a rice pudding in the oven and leave it to cook while we go out. It's half a mile's walk to the farm for the milk, but I'm sure you won't mind fetching it for me. Geraldine," she added, leading the way to the door,

" breakfast is usually at half-past seven. I cook, then. After that, there is just fruit and milk and cereal, so please do help yourself."

She walked out of the kitchen through a far door. Penny hesitated, uncertain as to what she should do.

" I will see that the other young lady has her breakfast," said Dilys Owen, laying aside her polishing cloths. " Do you now go to fetch the milk."

Miss Chart was outside in a paved yard. She led the way across it to a door set in a stone wall.

" This is our burgage," she said to Penny. " It's the local word for a garden, and I like it. And there is Tommy Owen, Dilys's husband, who keeps it tidy for me. There he is—over by the celery bed."

A bent old man with a face like a wise gnome straightened himself and came towards them.

" How's the sea to-day, Tommy ? " asked Miss Chart.

" Calm as a pond it is," said the elderly man. " I went down first thing to have a look at it."

" Not even a bit of a lop ? " demanded Miss Chart. She added to Penny, in a conspiratorial whisper, " Here, they say there's a bit of a lop when half a gale is blowing. A worse understatement I never did hear."

" It would be lovely to go out in a boat," urged Penny. " I've never been in a boat."

" Not even when coming from Africa ? " Miss Chart seemed surprised.

" We flew. It wasn't very exciting."

Tommy Owen was looking interested.

" Then this will be one of the young ladies you were expecting ? " he asked.

"I'm Penny," said the owner of that name. Remembering, she added shyly, "*Boreu da*."

Tommy was delighted. He shot out a spate of words that Penny did not understand at all.

"No good," said Miss Chart. "Penny has said all the Welsh she knows at present, and Dilys has only just taught her that. You do think it's a good morning for boating, Tommy? Well, perhaps we will go out."

"You should take a look at that lobster pot," said Tommy. "Who knows, but the biggest lobster in the bay may be waiting for you in it?"

"We haven't had much luck with lobstering this year," commented Miss Chart, "but perhaps Penny will improve it. We'll go out, just to look at the pot, as soon as she's fetched the milk." She turned to Penny. "You follow the path until you see the farm buildings, and then you make for the dairy. It's on the left. One of the Morgans is sure to be there. Tell them who you are—they know about the milk."

"Righto," said Penny. She swung the handle of the enamel can over her hand and began to walk away.

"And ask if Dai would like to come with us," called Aunt Pru, as she went off. "The *Ibis* will just about take four."

Penny followed the beaten track. It went straight through the spinney; every now and then she could see the silver of the brook sparkling through the trees. Except for the sound of water, it was very quiet, and a little bit eerie, so when she heard footsteps running behind her she turned sharply.

It was all right. The runner was Geraldine.

"Hello," said Penny companionably. "Are you coming for the milk too? Have you eaten your breakfast? You've been awfully quick."

"I only had a glass of milk," said Geraldine. "I wasn't hungry."

Penny began to walk on again.

"I had a scrummy breakfast," she remarked. "I had porridge and an egg and toast and marmalade and milk. I had it in bed, as I told you."

"You've evidently taken Miss Chart's fancy," commented Geraldine. Her tone was acid.

Penny bit her lip. "I don't really think much of eating in bed," she said. "The bed gets crumbly, and it's awkward to balance the tray."

"Don't tell Miss Chart that. She mightn't like it," counselled Geraldine.

Penny frowned.

"Of course I won't tell her. Why should I? It was very kind of her to bring my breakfast up because she thought I might be tired. And it was only this one time. I have to get up at the proper time to-morrow morning. Gerry . . . she is rather nice, isn't she? Unusual, but rather nice."

"I'm glad you think so," said Geraldine, in a voice that said that she herself did not.

"And this is a lovely place to be," insisted Penny. "I haven't seen it all, yet, but I can guess what it will be like, and everything will be fine. Did you know, Gerry, that there's a boat on the beach, and Aunt Pru is going to take us out in it to catch a lobster?"

"Personally," said Geraldine, "I think the place is

awful. I thought Uncle Ted's was bad, but this is worse. I'm wondering what we shall do with ourselves until this holiday is over."

Penny stood still.

"If you've nothing better to do," she suggested furiously, "you can read your French books. Your French report was pretty bad, wasn't it?"

Two red spots flamed in Geraldine's cheeks.

"Thank you," she said, "thanks very much. And when I want more of your advice, I'll ask for it."

She turned round and began to walk back along the path. Penny took a few steps after her.

"I'm sorry, Gerry. I didn't mean that at all. I can't think what made me say it."

Geraldine, too, turned. She faced her sister, hands clenched.

"Can't you? Well, I can. You said it because you wanted to hurt me, just like everybody else has since I left Kenya. You said it because you don't care about anything very much, so you don't mind being away from Mother and Daddy and home. Well, I don't mind. I don't mind being by myself. I'd be ashamed of myself if I was happy and laughing when I'd left everything I cared for. So there! And you can toady up to your Miss Chart and fetch the milk for her and go out in her boat. I want to be alone, and you needn't follow me, because that's that."

She dashed away through the spinney.

Penny turned slowly back towards the farm. The sunshine seemed to have gone out of the bright day. She felt tears pricking her eyes. She sniffed.

" I haven't forgotten Mother and Daddy," she muttered to herself. " They know I'd never forget them. But they'd want me to be happy here . . . and everybody is really so kind . . . and oh ! I do wonder why Gerry is like this ! I do, I do."

The tears clouded her eyes, so that she walked straight into a large youth who was coming down the path towards her.

" Hello," he said, stepping to one side. " Look where you're going, will you ? Have you seen a cow and a calf this way ? A white cow, she'd be."

Penny began to forget her sorrows.

" I haven't seen a cow, and I've come all the way from Yr Hafan."

The boy was studying her face with concern.

" I say," he remarked, " have you hurt yourself ? You've been crying."

" I think I had a fly in my eye," said Penny hastily. She rubbed her hand across her face to wipe the tears away.

" It doesn't look like a fly," said the boy.

" It's a fly if I say it's a fly, because I ought to know," said Penny firmly. She returned to the more interesting subject of the cow. " I don't think your cow could have come this way. If it's a white cow, I'd have noticed it, even if I wasn't looking for it."

" She calved in the night," explained the stranger. " We don't like our calved cows to go wandering off. If anything happens to them, or to the calves, we don't know where to look for them."

" Is it a cow from the Morgan's farm ? " asked Penny.

He nodded. " I'm Dai Morgan."

Penny thought that, for a boy, he looked nice. He had black hair waving from his forehead, bright blue eyes, and he was tall and sturdily built.

" I'm glad I met you," she told him. " I'm Penny Wilds, and I'm staying with Miss Prudence Chart. I'm fetching the milk. She asked me to tell you that she's taking the boat out for a lobster soon, and would you like to come too ? "

" I'd like to come well enough," said Dai slowly, " and I think I could, if it were not for this cow. If I can find her in time and take her back to the farm, I'll be along. Will you tell Miss Chart that ? "

" I will," promised Penny. He gave her a friendly grin and went on along the path.

The path came out on to a little, unfenced meadow. It was bordered on one side by a brook, where yellow-beaked ducks were dabbling, and on the other by a house, a barn, and a long, low building. Penny thought that this must be the dairy, and walked towards it.

Inside, the dairy was cool and wet. Churns stood to one side, with a cooling machine near them. A long slate shelf ran the length of the wall, and at it a stout woman was working butter with two wooden pats. She heard Penny's footsteps and looked round.

" *Boreu da*," said Penny politely, " I've come for the milk for Miss Chart."

The stout woman's face dimpled with a smile.

" *Boreu da*," she returned, " and is that all the Welsh you have ? "

" It is at present," admitted Penny, " because I only

came here last night and I haven't had time to learn any more. I'm Penny."

" I thought you might be," said the farmer's wife. " Bronwyn Morgan I am, and I've heard tell of you." She continued working the butter between the two wooden pats, both to mix in salt and to drain out whey. Penny was fascinated. After a few minutes, the woman wiped her hands. She took the can from Penny and filled it full of frothing milk before she replaced the lid firmly. " Always make sure the lid cannot slip," she instructed her. " Easy it is to upset milk if the lid's loose on the can."

Penny looked round the dairy.

" I do think you live in a lovely place," she said sincerely.

Mrs. Morgan laughed. " That's as may be. I like it well enough, but then, see you, it has always been my home. There are strangers who would find it lonely."

" I don't think I would," said Penny.

" There's plenty to do and plenty to see," agreed Mrs. Morgan. " That is, if you look for it with the right sort of eyes. Now, put down that can and wait while I finish this butter, and I'll take you into the barn and show you the twin calves that were born yesterday."

Penny hesitated.

" I'd love to see them, but Aunt Pru wants to make a rice pudding, and then we are going out in the boat."

" Then you'd best be home quickly," advised Mrs Morgan. " A good woman is Miss Chart, but never one to wait patiently. Come back another day and Dai will show you over the farm."

" I met Dai," said Penny. " He's coming boating with us after he's found the cow."

" Mind he does find that cow first then," said Dai's mother. She walked to the dairy door with Penny. " And here's another word for your Welsh," she added, as Penny walked away. " *Llaeth*. That's the milk you have in your can."

" *Llaeth*," repeated Penny, trying to thicken the *ll*s as Mrs. Morgan did.

" Not too bad," said the farmer's wife, and returned to her butter-making.

Penny hurried back to Yr Hafan as fast as she could. She had just enough breath left, when she came into the kitchen, to put the can on the table and say to Dilys Owen, " *Llaeth*."

" *Yr llaeth*," corrected Dilys. " *The* milk, like Yr Hafan, *the haven*."

Miss Chart called down the hall.

" Is that Penny back with the milk ? Did you ask Dai to come out in the boat ? Right. Then fetch a thick sweater and we'll be off. We don't want to miss the tide."

" A sweater ? " repeated Penny.

" A sweater," called back Aunt Pru. " It's never so hot out at sea."

CHAPTER SEVEN

BOATS AND LOBSTER POTS

EQUIPPED with thick sweaters, Penny and Miss Chart took the path to the beach. It was narrow, and here and there outcrops of rock had to be negotiated; in other places, brambles grew far out over the path. There were even a few ripe early blackberries, which Penny picked and ate with zest.

" Mind they're ripe," cautioned Aunt Pru. " I simply wouldn't know how to cope with tummy troubles."

" I never have tummy troubles," Penny assured her. " Aunt Clare used to say I had a stomach made out of cast iron. Look! There's a gorgeous spray of blackberries— simply gorgeous. Oh do look! There are seven . . . no, eight. You eat some, too. Try that very black one, there."

" As I haven't a cast-iron stomach myself," said Miss Chart, dryly, " I think I'd better decline."

She pulled up short and pointed. " See those ? " she murmured.

Penelope stopped short, too. She looked in the direction of the pointing finger. " Snakes! " she cried. " A whole nestful of them! "

" Not real snakes, just slowworms," corrected her aunt. " Real snakes—at least, the only real snakes we have in Britain—have a V-shaped mark on their heads.

They're adders, and are usually smaller than these slow-worms. There *are* adders in Wales, as well as these harmless creatures, so look carefully before you try to pick one up."

"I don't think I'd ever try to pick one up," confessed Penny. "I'd sooner stick to blackberries. Are you a naturalist? You do seem to know a lot about natural things."

"I've a smattering of knowledge about many things," Miss Chart assured her gravely. "And I love the wild life of these parts. There are two badgers in the woods, for instance. Sometimes, when I come back late at night, I see them in the gleam of the van headlights. I remember once that Mr. Brock Badger got in front of my van just at the bottom of that steep, narrow bit of the lane, and I had to follow him, in low gear, right to the top. He looked so comical, with his little bowed legs working as fast as they could. But that's enough about badgers and snakes. We shall find the tide catching up with us if we don't hurry. Come along. It's not much farther to the beach."

And it was not. The path opened suddenly on to a stretch of bare, striated rock that sloped quickly to shingle and then to gold-brown sand. The sand stretched for perhaps three hundred yards between great cliffs that were crowned with heather and bracken. The mouth of the little haven narrowed sharply, and there, just beyond it, breaking in one shining line of foam, was the sea.

"The tide has turned," said Miss Chart. "That is very satisfactory."

Penelope was staring around her.

" Is this yours ? Is it all your own ? "

" All my own as far as high tide mark," agreed her aunt. " Below that, the beach is common property. But there is no path to it, except the one through Yr Hafon land—although it is just possible to clamber from the big bay at the other side of the cliffs, over the boulders at the mouth of the inlet. It's rather risky, because the tide runs in very quickly here, at first. I should like you to promise me not to attempt it, Penny."

Penny nodded.

" Righto. I won't. Gosh ! " Her eyes had settled on something. " Gosh ! Is that your boat ? "

" That's the *Ibis*," said Miss Chart.

They scrambled carefully down the rock approach and made for the dinghy.

" What's an ibis ? "

" It's a bird. All the other boats in this class were given birds' names, so I called this one *Ibis*."

" I think it's an Egyptian bird," said Penny. " I'm not sure, but I think it is."

" You're quite right," said Aunt Pru. " In fact, unexpectedly knowledgeable." She walked up to the boat and began to inspect it.

" But an Egyptian bird ? " persisted Penny. " I mean, you might have had a buzzard. I mean, buzzards are unusual, but they are Welsh, aren't they ? "

" Yes, but I don't think a buzzard is a good bird for a boat, do you ? They're rather slow and heavy, in spite of being birds of prey. The *Ibis* isn't very fast, but she's faster than a buzzard."

Penelope walked around and also inspected the dinghy —the first one she had ever seen at such close quarters. It was clinker built, with narrow, varnished planks of wood running horizontally along its sides. It was perched on a carrier of metal, and that, in turn, was bolted to rubber-tyred wheels.

"No water in it, so no baling," commented Miss Chart. "I'll get the oars and the rowlocks and the outboard, and I hope young Dai appears soon, because, if he does not, we shall have to go without him."

"There's Geraldine," said Penny shyly. She was not sure that her sister would be a welcome substitute for the boy from the farm.

Miss Chart glanced round carelessly.

"Is she on the beach? I hadn't noticed her. Ask her if she would like to come out with us, by all means, Penny. Even if Dai does turn up, there is room for four."

She strode lightly towards a stout little shed that was tucked away at the foot of the cliff, took out a key, and opened the door.

Penelope ran across the shingle to Geraldine, who was sitting out of the sun with a book in her hands. Penelope regarded the book with horror, because she could see, at a glance, that it was Advanced French.

"Do put that away," she urged, "and come out to the lobster pot with us. It's a lovely boat, and it's going to be fun."

Geraldine stared sulkily at the *Ibis*.

"It looks rather small to me," she observed.

"Small? It's simply enormous when you're close up

to it. Aunt Pru says there's room for four, and she should know. Do come, Gerry. You can't sit here studying a school-book all day."

" Can't I ? " queried Geraldine. " I feel that I most certainly can. And, while we are on the subject, once and for all, will you *please* not shorten my name ! "

" I do think you're a pain, Geraldine," said her sister heartily, and then, before there could be a reply, raced away.

Miss Chart had carried an outboard motor from the shed and was tightening it on to the gunwale.

" Fetch the oars, will you, Penny ? " she asked. " And the rowlocks, too, if you can find them. They should be on the shelf with the fishing tackle. Be careful, and don't get hooks in your fingers."

The hut was an intriguing place, if there had been time to enjoy it. Bright-painted lobster-pot markers hung from nails, there were two green glass ones lying in a corner, and faded red sails were draped around the walls. Penny just took in these things, before she picked up the rowlocks from the shelf and gathered two stout oars from another corner. She hurried back to the dinghy.

" There are sails," she said. " Aren't we going to sail ? "

Miss Chart shook her head.

" Not to the lobster-pots. We sink them close under the cliffs, and it is much easier to reach them with the motor and a bit of rowing. I'll take you sailing, one day, but not just now. And that reminds me. You'd better put on a life-jacket. I don't usually bother with one unless I'm sailing, but, you never know. I should hate to have

to explain to your parents that you accidentally fell overboard and I wasn't able to fish you out again."

"I won't fall overboard," promised Penny.

"Put the oars in the bottom of the boat, blades pointing to the bow. They're easier to get at, that way. Rowlocks go there—in those brass-lined holes . . . that's right.
And fetch the jacket from the shed. You can't miss
it. It's a padded yellow one."

Penelope made another trip to the shed. She returned
with the life-jacket which was cold and damp and
bulky.

"Drop it along with the oars," directed Miss Chart.
"You needn't put it on till we are out at sea."

She had fastened the motor to her satisfaction and
now walked back from the dinghy and gazed up the path.

"It doesn't look as though Dai has finished his chores,"
she said. "Never mind. We can launch without him,
and maybe he'll turn up before we are afloat. How about
Geraldine ? "

"She's studying Advanced French," said Penny.

"How nice ! " commented Miss Chart. She sounded
relieved as she turned to the long, looped handle that
projected beyond the bow of the boat and to which a
thin hawser was fastened. She loosed the hawser.

"You don't know anything about boats, do you ? "
she asked casually. "I'll explain as we go along. If I
explain something you know already, it doesn't matter,
and it will save missing any important points. That's
the winch, the heavy thing there, with the hawser wound
on its drum. We use it to pull the *Ibis* above the tide
mark. This thing she's on, is her trolley. We're going

to push her down to the sea on it. Going down is easy."

She lifted up the looped handle and pushed, and the *Ibis*, on the wheels of her trolley, began to move towards the sea. Penny took hold of the handle and pushed as well.

"I like to go out just after the tide has turned," explained Miss Chart. "It's no trouble pushing the *Ibis* down to the sea, and if we come home on the tide, the sea brings her up the beach for us. As well as that, even on calm days like this, there's a nasty roller or two across the entrance at dead low tide. When there's a bit of a lop, it's definitely unsafe to go out until the tide is halfway up."

The rubber-tyred wheels ran easily over the firm sand. There was a gentle splash, and the first ripples lapped round the trolley.

"Hold it for a moment," said Miss Chart. She loosed the handle and began to roll her slacks up high, exposing very long, thin brown legs. "Your shorts are short enough," she observed. "You should be all right."

Together, they pushed the trolley farther into the sea. Suddenly, it was very heavy to push. Then, equally suddenly, the load lightened. Miss Chart sprang round to the side of the dinghy and steadied her away from the trolley. The little boat moved easily.

"She's floating," Miss Chart said. "Pull the trolley back pretty far up, Penny, and then leave it. We won't want to find it swept away when we come back."

Penny pulled the dripping trolley up the beach. She felt very much of a sailor as she left it there.

Aunt Pru had climbed over the side and was sitting

on the stern seat of the *Ibis*, with the outboard motor still cocked up out of the water, and an oar in one hand. With this, she propelled the dinghy near Penny. " In you come," she called, and in Penny went. In a moment she was sitting on the middle thwart, afloat.

" Can you row ? " asked Aunt Pru. Penny shook her head.

" Oh, well, we'll soon teach you. We usually row out a little way until there's enough depth to let the outboard down. Dai usually does that, but, as he isn't here, I'll take over."

" He *is* here, I think," said Penny.

Sure enough, Dai was racing down the beach, hardly stopping to roll up his slacks. Out of breath, he got into the boat. " Never thought I'd make it," he said, gasping.

" I reckon you waited for us to launch," said Miss Chart.

Dai picked up the other oar in a business-like fashion. He settled in the middle of the rowing thwart. " Climb on the prow," he suggested to Penny. " I can manage the oars better if I have the seat to myself."

" No. Let Penny take an oar," said Miss Chart. " She ought to learn to handle the oars. If you give one pull to three or four of hers, Dai, I daresay you will keep the boat straight. Sit beside Dai, Penny, and hold your oar with both hands. Dip the blade in the water a little behind you—that's right—now, lean back a bit, and pull."

Penny leaned back and pulled, and the *Ibis* sheered over to Dai's side of the boat. He put his own oar into the water. " Maybe she'll learn to row," he said briefly.

They rowed up and down the little harbour, as the tide

filled it. The *Ibis* zigzagged to and fro, as the unevenly-matched oarsmen pulled, but Penny only disgraced herself once, and that was when she lost her oar.

"Never mind," said Miss Chart, when she saw it floating, "it's time for serious business, anyhow." She lowered the outboard into the water, pulled a cord, and it began to buzz noisily. She steered the boat competently, chasing the oar until Dai shipped it again, and then they set out to sea.

"That's Crab Rock," she said, as they passed a blackly shining rock that just jutted from the sea. "It's our only real hazard. At high tide, it's completely covered, and we have to steer clear of it. When you start steering, remember that."

The motor carried the dinghy effortlessly out of the haven, and they made for the menacing cliffs to the right.

"There's one of the markers," exclaimed Dai, staring across the gentle sea. "Shut off the motor, Miss Chart, and I'll row us up to it."

There was a sudden silence when the motor stopped, and then Dai, taking both oars as a matter of course, began to row very close to the cliffs.

"Give me the boat-hook, Penny," said Miss Chart. She took the long pole, with the stout hook on the end, and gradually fished a bright scarlet marker buoy close to the boat. She dropped it in the bottom of the dinghy, on top of the life-jacket. "We forgot that," she said, beginning to haul in fathoms of yellow rope. "Never mind. It's far too wet to insist on your wearing it now. Here we come. Here's the pot. And—Dai! Penny has brought us luck! There's a lobster in it."

The wicker pot came slowly up to the surface and Miss Chart gathered it, dripping water, into the boat. Inside was something black and shiny that waved ineffectual claws.

"It's a lobster all right," agreed Dai. "Can you deal with it?"

"I'll try," said Miss Chart. She thrust a brown arm into the pot, grabbed the lobster by both claws, and brought it out.

"Here's a bit of string," said Dai. "Tie those claws out of the way."

Miss Chart tied the claws, laid the catch in the boat, and dropped the pot over the side. She paid out the rope until the marker floated again.

"There's still enough bait in the pot for another lobster," she said.

"Should be," agreed Dai. "I thought we baited up that pot enough for half a dozen lobsters."

"Perhaps we'll have another in the other pot."

But the other pot, brought to the surface and scrutinised, was empty.

The outboard took them easily back, past the place where Crab Rock was now hidden by the tide, and into the enclosed harbour. Penny's face fell. The sea trip had been quite marvellous, and far, far too short.

"Would you two people like to go on practising rowing?" said Miss Chart.

"Could we?" gasped Penny. It was a gasp of delight.

"I can trust Dai not to take you out of the haven. I think I can trust you, too, not to do anything he says not to, can't I?"

" Oh, you can, you can," breathed Penny. She remembered another person. " If Dai doesn't mind," she added, looking hopefully at the boy.

" You're sensible," said Dai briefly. " I don't mind taking you around."

" You'll beach the dinghy, then ? Drag it above tide level. There's a spring tide, and you never know if the wind will get up."

Miss Chart shut off the motor and tipped it up. She waited until the dinghy bumped gently on the sand beneath the waves. Dai steadied the boat with the oars while she leaped overboard, gathering up the lobster and the outboard, and waded back to dry sand.

" Come in before the tide turns," she called, as she left.

" We'll be in," promised Dai.

And, after an hour's blissful rowing practice about the harbour, he left Penny holding the *Ibis* while he ran up the sands for the trolley, slipped it neatly under the boat so that the little waves rode her on to it, and then, between them, they winched her safely home.

" I've never, never," said Penny, when the oars and rowlocks had been put away, " had such a wonderful day."

" We'll have to see that you have more while you're here," said Dai.

" Please, oh, yes," Penny said.

CHAPTER EIGHT

HOME TRUTHS

AT the end of the first week at the house by the sea, Penny was having a marvellous time. She knew everybody and chattered to everyone, from Mrs. Morgan at the farm to Davies the Post, using very freely the score or so of Welsh words she had picked up. She ran errands for Dilys Owen and prepared the *Ibis* for launching. She had even crewed when Miss Chart had set the sails of the little boat and taken her out far into the bay, where they ran gaily before a light wind, and tacked quietly to and fro. Everything was lovely.

She felt happy and important and probably was showing off a bit.

Geraldine did none of this. She spent a lot of time on the beach, because there she could find a place hidden behind rocks where she was away from everybody else. She took her books to her hiding place, but the results of her studies were not good. She brooded, and became even more difficult and silent. At Uncle Ted's home, although she would never have admitted it to herself, she had felt important, even if only because she knew that gentle Aunt Clare could be hurt and worried by the things she chose to say. This Aunt Pru, as Penny called her, was not worried by Geraldine at all. As far as

Geraldine could see, she hardly existed for Miss Chart. She was there at Yr Hafan; she was fed; she had the use of a neat bedroom. And that was all.

She felt that she was the chief actress in a tragedy, but when there was nobody to watch the play, being its star seemed to lack point.

That morning, Miss Chart was not at the breakfast table, but Penny was there first, acting very important.

" Aunt Pru's gone up to the mountain," she informed her sister, pulling a pan from the rack. " She told me to cook for us if I felt like it, or we could just have cereal for breakfast. I'm going to grill bacon. Shall I do some for you ? "

" Do you know how to grill bacon ? " demanded Geraldine cautiously. " You never cooked in Kenya."

" I can cook a lot of things now," said Penny confidently. " Aunt Pru taught me some, and Dilys Owen told me others. I can do Welsh rarebit and *bara brith* and Welsh cake on the griddle. And of course I can grill bacon. How many rashers, and do you want an egg as well ? "

Geraldine nodded. " What's *bara brith* ? " she inquired, " or did you make that up ? "

" It's a currant loaf. Good bread—*bara brith*. That's the Welsh for it. Actually, the only one I made wasn't exactly good, because it never rose at all. Aunt Pru said, ' feed it to the farm ducks ', and she hoped it wouldn't make them sink." Penny slashed four rashers of bacon expertly, put them in a pan, and placed the pan under the hot grill. " Talking of the farm reminds me," she said. " Would you go for the milk to-day ? It's not very far, and it's time you went up to the farm and met the Morgans."

Geraldine sat down at the table and waited for her breakfast. "Why should I?" she demanded.

"Well, they're nice," said Penny. "Especially Dai. That's why I want you to fetch the milk. Aunt Pru said Dai and I could take the boat around to the lobster-pot, only we have to go out before half-tide. Tide's at noon to-day, so what Dai thought was, if I'd get the *Ibis* ready as soon after breakfast as possible, he'd rush through his chores and we could be off. So you will fetch the milk, won't you?"

"I'll fetch it," promised Geraldine ungraciously. "I suppose it's quite all right that you two should take that boat out by yourselves? I'm rather surprised that Miss Chart suggested it."

"She wouldn't have done it if she hadn't been sure it would be safe," said Penny, turning the bacon. "But Dai's sixteen, you know, and pretty strong, and he's been helping Aunt Pru with her boat as long as he can remember. I hope we get a lobster. The last one was *gorgeous*."

She began to crack two brown-shelled eggs into the pan.

"Where's Miss Chart gone?" asked Geraldine idly. "It's very early for her to have gone out, isn't it?"

"I do wish you wouldn't keep saying 'Miss Chart', Gerry," complained her sister. "Why can't you say 'Aunt Pru', like I do? I know she wouldn't mind. She's gone up to her excavation. She often goes up. I can't think why, because it seems an awful waste of time when there are so many things to be done down here."

Geraldine stared.

" Her excavation ? "

Penny nodded. " Um. It's somewhere high in the hills. I think it was a Stone Age camp. I'm not very interested in Stone Age camps, you know, so I didn't ask much about it. All that sort of thing was so very long ago, and there are so many more interesting things to do to-day."

" I might have been interested," said Geraldine slowly.

Penny carried two plates containing crisp bacon and golden-centred eggs to the table. " Gosh," she said, " you haven't even poured the coffee. Never mind. It's on the stove. There's your bacon. Is it all right ? "

Geraldine nodded. She was still intent on this new aspect of Miss Chart's busy life.

" I wonder how she got the idea she'd like to excavate ? I suppose she's read books about it. I wonder if she's read the same books that I studied in Kenya."

" Ask her," advised Penny promptly. " She doesn't bite."

" I've never even been inside her room."

Penny giggled. " Aunt Pru's study ? I have. I like it. But do be sure you knock before entering, unless you've been invited. I barged in once when she was writing, and she nearly blew my head off."

Geraldine felt slightly cheered to know that Miss Chart could be stern with her young sister, if occasion demanded it. She ate her breakfast and enjoyed it, demanded directions to the Morgan farm, and set off with the milk can.

She followed the little path that Penny had first found

enchanting and now hardly noticed as she trod it. She, too, felt the silence of the woods close around her and that sudden sense of being very much alone. She walked through the woods quickly, and came out on to the clearing. A long, bedraggled sow, rooting near her feet, grunted at her as she advanced. Geraldine was not used to sows, or to any other farm animals, so she skirted the little meadow carefully, keeping as far away from the sow as she could. If she had walked across the beaten track that ran between turfs starred with daisies and butter-cups, she would have been seen from the dairy window where Mrs. Morgan and her son were standing, cleaning churns. As it was, she came quietly and unseen to the dairy door.

It was open, and she heard them talking.

" Off again in that boat ! " Bronwyn Morgan was say-ing. " Indeed, Dai, it's a farmer we're making of you, not a sailorman."

" The boat makes a nice change," said Dai. Geraldine heard water splashing as he rinsed a churn. " And we're not too busy on the farm just now."

His mother laughed. " Maybe it's young Penny you're interested in, more than the boat and the fishing ? "

Dai dumped the churn on the floor and picked up another one.

" Penny's a nice kid. She's not much to look at, but she's a good sport. The other one, though—Geraldine—she's pretty."

" Pretty is as pretty does," retorted his mother, " and I'd be sorry to see you turning your eyes on that one. Why, Dilys Owen was telling me she could not help hearing Miss Chart on the telephone, when the niece's husband asked her to take the girls. Terrible, she said it must have been, the way the older girl had carried on."

" She couldn't have told that if she didn't hear *all* the conversation," said Dai.

" She heard enough to know what I'm telling you is truth. She heard Miss Chart say that if her niece's health and happiness were at stake, she'd have the girls here for the holidays. If that doesn't mean she'd been a trial, you tell me what does ? "

" I think she's shy," said Dai quietly.

Bronwyn Morgan snorted.

Geraldine had listened, without meaning to eavesdrop. She had clattered the milk can a little, to warn them that she was there. Then, when her own name was mentioned, she had stood still, pinned to the ground with horror. She listened, and her pulses drummed in her head so that she could hardly breathe. Somehow, she managed to slip away from the door and behind a jutting wall. She stood there, clutching the milk can, staring in front of her. So that's how Miss Chart and everybody else in the district thought of her. That's how her loneliness and grief for her home and her parents had been misconstrued.

She wanted to fling herself on the ground and howl out her sorrow like a small girl, but she was nearly fifteen, and could not do that. She had to master herself, to make herself face the abominable woman who had been talking to Dai in the dairy, to go back there and fetch the milk, and behave as if she had heard nothing she was not meant to hear.

She did this, but, because she was so hurt and uncertain, she was less cool and controlled than usual. She did not seem so much offhand and unfriendly, as shy. She introduced herself quietly, and asked for the milk.

Dai turned his head from the corner where he was working.

" Penny's got you to do her job while she gets the boat ready ? " he asked. " That's good of you. Tell her I'll be down in half an hour. I've nearly finished here."

Bronwyn Morgan poured milk into the can.

" And what do you do with yourself while the others are out fishing ? " she inquired.

Geraldine hesitated. " I study. I'm not very good at school, and I'm trying to catch up."

" No way that is to spend a holiday," declared the farmer's wife, fixing the lid tightly. " Leave your books and go out in the boat with the others."

It was almost the first time anybody near Yr Hafan had seemed to consider Geraldine at all.

" I'm afraid of the sea," she told Mrs. Morgan truthfully.

Bronwyn handed the filled can to the girl. " Well, we all of us have our own likings," she observed, " and I cannot say that mine goes for a boat."

Geraldine walked away from the dairy, thankful that she had been able to face the Morgans as though nothing had been overheard. She walked straight across the path and the sow moved automatically as she approached. Behind her departing back, Mrs. Morgan said slowly, " Well, I don't know. That's the first time I've met the girl, but you may have the truth of it, Dai. It may just be that she is shy."

Geraldine slipped as quietly as she could into the house and left the can of milk on the kitchen table. Then out she went and back into the garden. Tommy Owen was working in the burgage, but she walked past him without seeing him. Tommy turned his head and stared after her and then spat on the ground, " Sassenach ! " said Tommy Owen, using the old Gaelic name for the Saxon invaders and a word of great dislike.

Geraldine followed a narrow trampled path that led down to the stream. She sat on a mossy rock and stared unseeingly into the dancing water. She gulped. Everything about her felt heavy and dull. Words drummed in her ears. Mrs. Owen, listening to Miss Chart's conversation on the telephone, misinterpreting it, and then spreading the results all over the place. Everyone, at the farm and in the village, must have been told that she had been sent away because she was " terrible." Because her real aunt could not live with her. Davies the Post must know. Davies the Butcher probably knew. So must the telephone engineer and the man who delivered the bread. Geraldine understood local customs quite shrewdly, and she knew that every bit of gossip was retold avidly. She fairly cringed as she thought how good a subject for such gossip she had been.

But it wasn't true, she thought, with her head in her hands. It wasn't true. She wasn't terrible and impossible to live with. It was just that she had realised that even her parents could let her down, and she had to learn to be hard and not hurt by ever loving anybody else. That was why she wanted to be Geraldine and not Gerry. Gerry had been young and silly and confiding, and had been sent away from home in spite of it, so there was nothing for it but to grow hard.

She rubbed her eyes, scrambled to her feet, and began to move towards the distant sound of the sea. Her mouth was set in its harsh line.

Even Penny had deserted her for strangers. There wasn't anything or anybody she loved. She didn't care what any of them said. She'd just take as little notice of them as possible, work at her books, and then, one day, when she had made a name for herself and was famous, she would coolly patronise these people who were so dreadful to her now. Miss Chart and the little excavation she was playing with up in the hills ! Geraldine meant to become a real archæologist some day—and then it might be fun to show Miss Chart her mistakes.

She came out on the beach. She must have spent a long time sitting by the stream, because the *Ibis*, with Dai controlling the outboard and Penny dangling her legs over the prow, was coming slowly into land. She could hear their laughing voices over the water. She could not bear to meet them, so she slipped away between high rocks.

That was where she found the baby seal.

CHAPTER NINE

THE BABY SEAL

WHEN Dai beached the boat, Geraldine was standing breathlessly waiting for him.

"Do come," she urged, "please do come! There's
something behind those rocks, and it's alive and it's
crying. I don't know what to do to help it."

"We'll come," said Dai quietly. "Give me a minute
to make the *Ibis* safe. The tide is still rising."

"Is it a dog?" asked Penny, carrying up oars and
rowlocks. "No? Perhaps it's a calf or a sheep or a goat
that's fallen over the cliff?"

"I know what calves and goats look like," said
Geraldine impatiently. "This isn't anything like that.
It hasn't any legs."

"It sounds like a seal," said Dai.

"But it cries," objected Geraldine.

"Seals do make a noise, though I wouldn't call it
crying," he told her, and then, looking up the beach, he
saw a tall, slender figure descending to the sands. "Here's
Miss Chart," he added. "She'll be sure to know what
your creature is."

Miss Chart strode up to them with her long, easy lope.

"I thought I might be back before you started," she
called. "When I got to the dig, there was a message from

Geraint saying that he couldn't come, and there wasn't much more that I could do without help, so I've taken a day off. Shall we go out again in the *Ibis* ? "

Geraldine forgot that Miss Chart was reserved with her. " Do come and see what it is I've found," she begged. " It's ill or injured, I'm sure of that. Please come and help."

" What is this thing and where ? " demanded Miss Chart.

" Dai thinks it's a seal," said Penny. " I hope it is. I've heard of seals, but I've never seen one."

Geraldine led the way. " Here. Behind these tall rocks. That's it. The furry, whitish creature."

She ran across a narrow strip of shingle and crouched beside the something. It was wet and furry and grey-white. It was about three feet long and so fat that it must have been just as wide as it was long. It had two enormous sad brown eyes, two big front flippers, two small back ones, and a thick tail. It wriggled towards Geraldine surprisingly quickly, opened a large mouth so that tiny, sharp teeth showed in it, and made a wailing noise that was partly a bark and partly a cry.

" It's a baby seal," said Miss Chart.

" It's very wet and cold and hungry. What can we do for it ? " asked Gerry.

" I don't think it's very hungry," Miss Chart said. " It looks too fat to have been starved. And I don't think it feels cold. It's unusual to find a baby seal at this time of year. Most of them are born in December, and I've often come across seal mothers feeding their calves at that time."

" This one hasn't a mother," said Geraldine, with a catch in her voice.

Penny touched the baby seal gently. It wriggled around towards her and again made the strange, barking cry.

" I think the best thing to do is to leave the young thing," said Miss Chart. " Quite likely, its mother will come back to it. I don't think we could keep it alive, anyway. We could try a bottle, with cow's milk, but seal milk is far richer than that, and the baby wouldn't flourish on it."

" And if the mother seal doesn't come back? What shall we do then?" Geraldine's concern was genuine.

Miss Chart sighed. " I suppose the best thing to do— and the kindest in the long run—would be to leave it here. The sea will take it away in due course."

" You mean leave it to die ? " Geraldine cried fiercely.

" Lots of creatures die every minute of the day, Geraldine. It's a natural process, and need not be terrible."

Geraldine rose to her feet. " I won't let it die ! I won't ! " she declared, clenching her hands.

Miss Chart looked at her curiously.

" You'll have great difficulty in keeping it alive. As I said, seal milk is far richer than cow's milk, and even if you did succeed in rearing the small thing with cow's milk and a bottle, it might never be strong or healthy enough to exist in competition with other creatures."

The little seal urged its fat body forward on those stout flippers. Penny put out a hand and touched its wet head, and it gave that queer, moaning bark.

" Seals eat fish, don't they ? " asked Geraldine. " Well,

then. Why not go out in the boat and catch some for it?"

" 'Twouldn't eat fish," objected Dai, who probably knew more about animals than the others did. " Look at its teeth. They're tiny. No. This seal is still a sucking seal."

" It wants its mother," finished Miss Chart.

Geraldine knelt tenderly by the seal. She stared up defiantly.

"Mothers aren't much good. I suppose this one's mother doesn't care what happens to her baby. I suppose she's gone off and left it. It's all nonsense that mothers are always kind and look after their children."

Penny exclaimed, in a shocked voice, " Gerry! Our mother isn't like that."

Geraldine's mouth twisted. " Isn't she? Well, no. She didn't exactly desert us. She just sent us away."

Miss Chart stared down at the bent, fair head. The bitterness in the girl's voice had taken her by surprise. She said, slowly and thoughtfully, " Let's give this particular mother a chance. For all we know, she's waiting in the bay, wishing we would all go away and leave the coast clear for her to come out of the water and feed her baby. I suggest that we walk back to the house and have some coffee. Then we'll come back, and if the baby really has been deserted, we'll plan what to do about it."

" That's a good idea," said Dai, nodding energetically. " The little seal will be all right if we leave it—it's just above high water. And if the mother doesn't come back to feed it, we'll walk up to the farm and I'll find one of the bottles we rear the orphan lambs with, and we'll see if the animal will take milk out of that."

" Do you really have orphan lambs ? " cried Penny, clasping her hands. " Really ? And you bring them up on a bottle by the kitchen fire ? I've read about that, but I wasn't sure that it happened."

" It's Mother who's soft about the lambs," explained Dai, as though rather ashamed that farming people should be so sentimental. " They can be a bother when they grow up, if they're reared as pets."

" I thought it was your own lamb that took to climbing the stairs and eating the bedclothes," said Miss Chart mildly.

" What ? A lovely lamb ! " exclaimed Penny. " Where is it now ? "

" With the rest of the flock, I imagine," said Aunt Pru promptly.

" Well, you couldn't bring up an orphan lamb and then eat it, could you ? " said Penny definitely, and nobody argued about this.

Miss Chart stared down at the seal thoughtfully. " What do we do if the seal has been deserted, and Geraldine manages to rear it ? I hardly fancy a pet seal in the house."

Geraldine gazed down into the great brown eyes of the seal.

" I suppose we should have to let it go. It wouldn't be happy in a house. Things aren't happy where they don't belong. And anyhow, we couldn't take it back to London. There isn't room in Uncle Ted's house."

" I couldn't look after it, either," said Miss Chart, leading the way back towards her home. " You see, almost as soon as you people have gone back to school, I'm leaving Yr Hafan myself."

Penny slid a sticky hand into her aunt's.

"Must you leave it? It will seem worse when we have to go away, if we know you won't be here, either."

Miss Chart smiled, and squeezed the sticky hand.

"I shall come back, and you must come back, too."

Penny gave a wild leap for joy.

"May we? May we really? That's marvellous. It *is* marvellous, isn't it, Gerry?"

Geraldine knew that Miss Chart was watching her, still with that curious, impersonal gaze.

"It would be nice to come back," she mumbled.

"Though I don't see why you should think so," added her sister truthfully. "You really don't make the best of Yr Hafan, Gerry. You don't go swimming or climbing or anything. Why, I don't believe you've even been out in the *Ibis*, yet."

"I'm not used to the sea," said Geraldine lamely.

"I'd show you how to row the boat," put in Dai encouragingly. "I'd teach you the way of it, and I'd be careful we didn't go outside the haven. That is, if Miss Chart would trust me with her boat."

"I know you're safe with it, Dai," said the owner of the boat, cheerfully. "If you'd like to, by all means take it out again and show Geraldine the ropes. She may find herself enjoying it, after all."

They all trooped into the big kitchen and Miss Chart poured coffee for the four of them and extra cups for Dilys and Tommy Owen, and Davies the Post, who drew up in his little red van just then. There were two air-mail letters from Kenya, and the girls grabbed them quickly.

" Daddy hasn't sold our farm yet," announced Penny, while Geraldine read her own letter. " He says he's hopeful, but not to count on it too much."

" Is your father a farmer ? " asked Dai. " I didn't know there were farms and farmers out there in Africa."

" He chiefly farms coffee," admitted Penny, " but there are some animals as well."

" We couldn't grow coffee here, I suppose," said Dai solemnly.

" Too wet, and not enough sun," Miss Chart said briskly, standing up again. " Never mind, Dai. We grow beautiful early potatoes in Wales, not to mention some of the finest mutton and wool in the world. And now, shall we go back to the beach and see what is happening to the little seal ? "

They trooped back, and, when they came to the beach, threaded a way between the rocks very quietly.

The seal was still there, but it was not alone.

Another seal—a simply enormous seal—was lying on the wet sand, just clear of the ripples that broke lazily behind it. The baby seal was snuggled up between its flippers. They could hear the noise it made as it sucked.

Miss Chart put a finger to her lips and drew back out of sight.

By and by, there was the scraping sound of something heavy being dragged over the shingle. The mother seal was going back to the sea, dragging herself laboriously. She flopped into the water, dived under the first wave, and then came upright. Geraldine, peering from behind her rock, could see the big seal's white face gazing at her baby, and then, satisfied that it was safe, she dived again, and did not surface for a long time.

The baby seal was sleeping peacefully, with a milk mark round its mouth.

Geraldine felt Miss Chart close to her.

" You see, the mother wasn't so bad after all, Geraldine," she said. " She just knew what was best for her baby."

Geraldine glanced at her, startled.

" Some mothers," she shot out suddenly, " do stay with their children. If the children have to go away, they go with them."

" If they can," said Miss Chart firmly. She hesitated, began to say something more, and then thought better of it. She called to Dai instead. " If you really mean to give Geraldine that lesson in managing the boat, Dai," she said, " better go now. The tide is right, and the sea is like a millpond."

" Come along," said Dai to Geraldine, " I may not be able to spare the time, another day. Will you give a hand with the trolley, Penny ? "

" I'll come with you, if you like," said Penny promptly. " I daresay I'd better come, in case Gerry gets seasick or thinks she's going to fall overboard."

" I'm going swimming," said Miss Chart. " Why don't you swim with me, Penny ? "

Penny thought this over. " I don't know which to do. I love boating and I love swimming. I think perhaps I'll swim, because I've been out in the *Ibis* once to-day already. Are you sure you'll be all right without me, Dai ? "

" I've been all right without you often enough before
you came here," retorted the Welsh boy indignantly.

Geraldine waded into the lukewarm water and he
helped her scramble over the side of the boat. He settled
himself on the rowing thwart with Geraldine at his side.
He pulled away strongly from the beach and then Penny,
watching critically, saw her sister take one oar. She saw
the boat begin to turn in a circle until Dai corrected the
difference between one strong and one weak oarsman.

" I never thought Gerry would go out with Dai," she
remarked, pulling on her bathing cap.

Miss Chart had also been watching the boating lesson.
She was frowning a little; then she shrugged her
shoulders and said, cryptically, " Oh, well. I shall have
to go through with it."

Penny was not meant to hear this, but she did.

" Go through with what ? " she asked.

" A duty," said Aunt Pru gravely. " A duty that I've
only just recognised."

" Sometimes duties can be a nuisance," said Penny,
beginning to splash into the water. Miss Chart followed
her.

" The water is really warm," she said. " That's how
I like it, for swimming. And, before I forget, Penny, and
in case Geraldine comes in after I've gone up to the
house, ask her to come to my study, will you ? I want
to talk to her."

" It's all right, isn't it ? " said Penny anxiously, wondering if her sister had been obnoxious behind her back.

" What shouldn't be all right about a talk ? " asked
her aunt lightly.

CHAPTER TEN

LECTURE BY MISS CHART

PRUDENCE Chart sat at the desk in her study. On the desk was a list that she had been filling in meticulously, but when Geraldine tapped at the door, she wasn't working on it. She was frowning across the papers with an air of abstraction.

"I wouldn't bother with the girl," she said to herself, in a grumbling way. "I wouldn't bother at all, but she seemed so desperately unhappy. Perhaps Clare never realised. I never did, until I saw her with the seal."

And then she called, "Come in," in answer to Geraldine's tap.

Geraldine had more colour in her cheeks than usual. Her eyes were bright and her dress rumpled. It looked as though the skirt of her cotton dress had got wet, and had then dried in the sun.

"I believe you enjoyed your rowing lesson," said Miss Chart, taking all this in.

Geraldine was looking round the room shyly. Her eyes travelled from the packed bookshelves, the glass-covered specimen cases, to the comfortable easy chair on the hearth and the wide desk on which was a bowl of roses as well as paper and pens and a telephone.

"I did enjoy it," she said, "it was good fun and Dai says he thinks I'll learn to row quite well. I got my dress wet when we brought the boat in, but I can rinse it out and iron it myself."

" You ought to wear shorts," said Miss Chart.

Geraldine flushed a little.

" Aunt Clare did offer to buy me some, but I refused."

" I daresay I could lend you a pair," offered Miss Chart. " You're fairly large for your age, and I'm very thin. They are just khaki shorts—nothing at all glamorous. I'll find an extra pair for you." Then she added abruptly, " You weren't very kind to your Aunt Clare, were you, Geraldine ? "

Geraldine saw two brown eyes regarding her coolly and knowledgeably.

" No, I wasn't," she mumbled.

Miss Chart began to light a cigarette.

" My niece Clare," she pronounced, " is a gentle, sweet, and feminine woman. Now I'm none of those things. I am neither sweet nor gentle, and sometimes I doubt that I am very feminine. I'm tough." She blew a spiral of smoke, and went on. " You are probably wondering what is the point of all this. Well, what I am trying to say to you is quite personal, and I would not have said it at all if I had not just realised how badly you have resented being sent away from home."

Geraldine bit her lip and did not reply.

" You see," Miss Chart continued, " being tough, I am not likely to be upset by any way you choose to take this lecture."

" You can't alter the fact that Mother and Father did send me away," muttered Geraldine.

" I *can* try to make you see some sense," retorted Miss

Chart vigorously. " Goodness, Geraldine, you must know that Kenya is in a very ticklish situation. Anything might happen there. The whole country is in a ferment, and while I hope it will settle down and that everything will turn out well because I have many good friends in Africa, it may not happen that way. Your parents were right to send their young girls out of the country. You might have been in danger : you would surely have been an added responsibility and even an embarrassment. But why you had to decide that sending you to England meant that your parents no longer cared for you, I just do not know. They are probably missing you just as much as you miss them, and I'm sure your mother has shed a few tears over your letters, just as I've seen Penny weeping a little when she gets hers."

" Perhaps you're right," said Geraldine slowly.

" I know that I'm right," returned Miss Chart. " I know how the mother mind works, whether it's animal or human. Your mother is perhaps consoling herself that you are having a marvellous time over here and that you'll have plenty to tell one another when you meet again. And you could have a marvellous time, you know. All you are doing by this attitude of yours is losing a lot of fun."

Geraldine flushed. " I don't think that's very kind," she said.

" I told you that I wasn't kind," returned the older woman. " I told you that I was tough. Anyhow, that's the end of my lecture, and I hope you will think it over."

Geraldine stood up. She walked over to the mantelshelf and began to finger a little figure that stood there. It was a queer little figure, shining dull gold, with two red stones for eyes in a rudimentary face.

" I've never got on with people as easily as Penny does." She spoke, slowly and with difficulty. " Penny makes friends awfully easily. I don't. And I did hate leaving all the things I was doing in Kenya."

" You had a dig," said Miss Chart.

Geraldine nodded. " How did you know ? "

" Penny told me. I was very interested, because it's my own line."

" Penny told me you had a dig, as well. She said it was a Stone Age camp.

Miss Chart nodded. " It is Stone Age, I think. Neolithic, probably. We'll soon know. Wales is absolutely littered with traces of primitive man, and I am not expecting any extraordinary find. Just the usual traces of man's way of life at that time—his arrangements for cooking, what he cooked, and how he caught it."

" It's not a building ? " asked Geraldine dubiously.

Prudence Chart laughed.

" Goodness, no ! I think that at its best it was a collection of stone beehive huts. We're investigating what looks to have been the largest one and, up to the present, there has been little of great interest, except an unusual dearth of flint."

" Why flint ? " inquired her listener.

Miss Chart sighed.

" Before the Iron Age, man depended a great deal on flint. He had to have something hard to make and sharpen his weapons. Flint was the answer, but there was little flint in Wales. So, even in those early times, trading began, men bringing flint from one side of this island to the other. They'd exchange it for something that they hadn't got locally, of course. Gold, perhaps, because there are many traces of little gold mines in the Welsh hills, and they were worked until Roman times, and after." She began to light another cigarette, and added, "But all this is childish stuff, Geraldine. If you've tried excavating on your own, you should have read about it, first."

The girl flushed.

"I have read some of it. Mother used to bring me books from the library, in Nairobi, but they didn't specialise in archæological books. Besides, there just weren't many books on the subject."

"The untrained worker can do much damage in the field," remarked Miss Chart, dryly.

Again Geraldine flushed.

"I don't think I did any harm," she said in a rush. "Really, I hadn't time to do much. It was just that one day, when I'd ridden rather farther than I usually did, there was a sudden storm. I could see it piling up, and I made for shelter. There was a ridge of hills nearby and I rode up a rift. At one side, there was a cave, so I waited in that. It was quite big and dry and I looked about while the rain came down. I noticed some queer scratches on the walls. I told Daddy about them, but he said probably bushmen had made them. I didn't think so, though. They looked like etchings—etchings of animals, only very worn. So I coaxed Mother to bring me a book about archæology and the things that have been found in caves, and after that I went back to my place and began digging up the floor of the cave."

"Interesting," commented Miss Chart. "Did anything turn up?"

Geraldine laughed. She looked at the little statue that she was still holding.

"Teeth," she admitted, "and one or two bones. What I'd been expecting was something like this."

"A thing like that," said Miss Chart, looking at the figurine with something like affection, "is the sort of thing only found at the sites of lost civilisations. It is definitely not a product of the unskilled people who once lived in caves. Actually, I dug it up myself, at Ur."

Geraldine gazed from the tiny golden figure to Miss Chart.

"It's real," she whispered.

Miss Chart laughed. "That depends on what you mean by real. The gold is genuine, and the figure isn't a modern copy. It may be an ancient copy of a still older statue, though. Quite a number of statuettes like it have been catalogued. Still, whatever else I may find, and whatever I have found since I came across the little god you're holding, it will be the most precious to me. The first find. I imagine the first is always the most precious one."

Geraldine replaced the figure carefully. She went on looking at it, because that way her back was turned to its owner. She was having to readjust her ideas about Miss Chart. She felt herself going hot with shame. To think that at one time she had felt slightly patronising towards a woman who had seemed to be nothing more than a good cook and a good sailor of boats !

" I suppose you are famous," she muttered.

Miss Chart's eyes twinkled.

" When even a budding young archæologist like your-self had never heard of me ? " she inquired demurely.

Geraldine sketched a gesture, which was meant to include Yr Hafan, the sandy cove, the brook and the boat.

" I thought all you wanted was this."

" I have to earn a living to come back to this," said Miss Chart quietly.

Geraldine turned to her. " But you do love excavations and archæology ? "

" Oh, yes. One would never be any good at anything, unless one wanted to do it, would one ? " Then she added, gravely, and as though she had read Geraldine's thoughts about cooking, " And you'd be surprised how useful having Yr Hafan as a background can be. In an emergency, I can turn out an excellent meal with the aid of a wood fire and a flat stone. And river crossings never bother me. I just remember the wash round Crab Rock when the tide is turning, and go ahead with circum-spection."

" I wish I could do that sort of thing some day," said Geraldine wistfully.

" Nothing to stop you, is there ? " asked Miss Chart briskly. " The necessary qualifications—besides an end-less patience—are a degree in history and the ability to speak a few extra languages. But don't go away with the idea that a dig is a glamorous affair and that worthwhile finds come to light every day. They don't. A dig is often sheer slow grinding, with little to show for it at the end. You'd better come up with me to Cader Mawr and see what I mean."

" To Cader Mawr ? To your own dig ? " Geraldine sounded excited.

" My own dig," agreed Miss Chart. " It's just a wee bit awkward to reach, and there's at least a mile to scramble and climb after we leave the van. Are you game for that ? "

" I'm game," said Geraldine.

" Remind me to find those shorts for you," said Miss Chart. " You'd never reach Cader Mawr in a dress."

A tap came on the door and Penny poked her head in. She was a little worried because her sister had been closeted in the study for such a long time, and she was not sure that the conversation taking place could be a pleasant one.

" I thought perhaps you'd forgotten about lunch," she said diplomatically, " shall I put the potatoes on to boil ? "

Geraldine took no notice of this.

" Penny," she burst out, " what do you think ? I'm going up to the dig ! "

Penny blinked. This was unexpected.

" When can I start ? " her sister went on, turning to Miss Chart. " To-morrow ? Do say I may come to-morrow."

" We could put in a few hours to-morrow," agreed Miss Chart. " I was let down this morning by the student who has been helping me. Yes. If you can be up for breakfast at seven o'clock to-morrow morning, Gerry, we'll go up to the dig. And don't expect too much, because Stone Age excavation is seldom thrilling."

" And what about me ? " demanded Penny, taking all this in.

Aunt Pru smiled. " Do you want to come and excavate too ? "

" I don't think I do," said Penny slowly. " I suppose it's all very interesting, but when there's such a lot of live things to do with live people, it seems a bit silly to waste time with dead ones. At least, I don't mean *you're* silly," she added hastily, " but just that it doesn't appeal to me. May I go fishing, if Dai can spare the time ? "

" Only if Dai can spare the time to go out with you," said Aunt Pru firmly. " I mean that, Penny. No trying to take the *Ibis* out by yourself."

" I hope he'll be able," said Penny. " I know he likes coming out, and even if there's a lot of work on the farm, Mrs. Morgan says while he's still at school he ought to have some school holidays. So as long as Dai washes down the dairy and takes care of the churns and cleans out the cowshed, he can do as he likes."

" It sounds like a full programme to me," commented Miss Chart.

" I like Dai," said Penny, with the frankness of the twelve-year-old. " I like him very much. I think he likes you, too, Gerry. He told me you were better in a boat than he thought you'd be."

Geraldine blushed rosily at this moderate praise. Aunt Pru saw the blush, and asked, with just a touch of humour, " Are you sure you don't want to change your mind and stay here to go boating, Gerry ? "

" I did love trying to row," said Geraldine quietly. " I'd like to learn the proper way to tackle an excavation, too. If you don't mind, I'll come to the dig to-morrow."

" Well, there'll be lots more days when you can come out in the *Ibis*," said Penny consolingly. " We've only been here ten days, and school doesn't begin again for another six weeks. Isn't that marvellous ? "

For the first time, Geraldine realised that it might be, and said, " Yes."

CHAPTER ELEVEN

THE DIG AT CADER MAWR

MISS Chart drove the red van expertly along a lane that twisted away from the sea and Yr Hafan, into the hills. Water ran gaily at the side of the lane, ferns hung lushly down the steep banks, and always the hills came closer and closer.

" They look like real mountains," said Geraldine, as the red van climbed slowly in low gear.

" They are real mountains," said Miss Chart. " The middle one is Snowdon—our highest Welsh mountain."

Geraldine remembered the steep white slopes of Mount Kenya that must have towered twice as high as these Welsh mountains, but she did not talk about it. Aunt Pru, however, seemed to guess her thoughts.

" Mountains," she observed, " are comparative. England and Wales—or perhaps I should say Britain and include Scotland and Ireland—are small countries. I think they'd be a little top-heavy if they had mountain ranges as big as those of Africa or America. Now, don't tell me that the Swiss mountains are high. I know it. And I know that Switzerland is a small country, too ; only it happens to be a country cut out of the middle of Europe and not an island set in the sea."

She steered the van slowly round a bend that doubled back on itself, and when they rounded the corner the lane came out on the side of a steep hill and lost all pretence of being a made road. Still, it went on, a stony track that led along the side of the hill, and which must have led upwards still, because the engine ground away stolidly in low gear.

" This is nearly as far as we can take the car," said Miss Chart. " We'll leave it at Jenny Jones's cottage and then we'll have to footslog. You can see the cottage now. There. See the little chimneys sticking up against the sky ? "

Geraldine strained her eyes to look ahead of her, and there, crouched close against the hillside, she could just make out a whitewashed cottage.

" But why should anybody want to live up here ? " she asked. " It's so far away from everywhere. How do they get food ? Or is there another way to reach it ? "

" There is another way," said Miss Chart, " I'd use it, but it means going about fifty miles along the main road until we come to it. That's even slower for me than using this track. And Jenny lives here because it has been her home all her life. Her husband was a shepherd ; he looked after the sheep in these hills. When he died, she did come down from the hills and lived with her daughter for a time, but it nearly broke her heart. She was used to the mountains, and the loneliness and the freedom. So she came back to her cottage. She keeps bees and sells the honey in our town. She also makes quilts—the old Welsh quilts that so few people know how to make to-day.

I daresay, if she takes a fancy to you, Jenny will show you how to quilt."

As she talked, the car had drawn closer and closer to the cottage, until it was driven right in front of it, where it could stop, and they could both get out. Miss Chart jumped out first, and stretched.

" Stiff? " she asked Geraldine.

"Bumped to pieces," said Geraldine promptly.

"Wait until we start the last part of the climb," warned Aunt Pru. " That's worse."

An old, old woman wearing a long black skirt, a gay cotton blouse, and a mobcap on her head, came to the cottage door. Miss Chart called out, " *Boreu da.*"

" *Boreu da,*" said Geraldine shyly.

The old woman replied in rapid Welsh, and in Welsh, although more slowly, Miss Chart answered her. Geraldine knew that questions were being asked about herself, and felt uncomfortable, but finally Jenny Jones walked up to her, wiped her hand on her spotless apron, and held it out to the girl. They shook hands heartily, and Geraldine felt that the questions asked must have been answered satisfactorily.

Miss Chart led the way from the cottage. It was a wild track that climbed the hillside rapidly.

"I think this is really the dried-up bed of a stream," she explained, as they climbed. "Probably, in wet weather, it foams with water. It was quite a feat getting our kit to the top of it the first few times we came, but we've rigged up a shelter now, and our tools stay up at the Caer."

She paused for breath, and they both looked back at the countryside they had left behind them. For the first time, Geraldine realised just how high they had climbed.

Below them the lush green lowland edged the sea in a ribbon of emerald. The sea itself was darkest blue. Here and there whitewashed walls broke the pattern of blue and green.

"That's Yr Hafan," said Miss Chart, pointing downward. "You'll have to take my word for it, because I doubt if you can distinguish it yourself."

"There's a tiny boat on the water," exclaimed Geraldine. "There. Quite close to land. That might be Dai and Penny, going out fishing."

"If it is, they'll be considerably cooler than I am," said Miss Chart. She mopped her forehead with a large handkerchief.

"You talked Welsh with Jenny Jones, Aunt Pru," said Geraldine.

"But of course!" said Miss Chart, trying not to show her surprise and pleasure at the "Aunt Pru." "Why should I not? This is my home, and I am Welsh on my mother's side."

"Penny knows a lot of Welsh words," said Geraldine.

"It's not a hard language to learn, but then, I grew up knowing how to speak it. It's a purer language than English. Mainly Celtic, of course, with quite a lot of Latin in it to mark the three hundred years that the Romans spent in British Britain. It was Welsh Britain, then, because the Welsh are the descendants of the original Britons, but I'm sure you know about all that. Anyhow, Welsh is Welsh, with a touch of Latin, as I said before, while English is a thoroughly mongrel tongue— Celtic, Saxon, Roman, Norman, the lot. Perhaps this accounts, in some part, for its peculiar spelling."

"Welsh spelling looks very peculiar to me," said Geraldine.

"I'll have to teach you to pronounce the Welsh alphabet, and then you'll find that it is not. And now, we've no more time to stand discussing Welsh, or looking down on my home—Yr Hafan—The Haven. Come along. When we've climbed the shoulder of the hill, we're over the worst of it. There's another half mile to go then, but it's steady climbing."

The hill rose before them and, as Geraldine plodded up the short springy turf, she thought that she would never get to the top. But even Welsh hills have their peaks and, suddenly, they were over the crest of this one, over its shoulder, and looking down on a warm hollow where grey stones were jumbled in the heather. A girl and a young man were working at one jumble of stones.

Miss Chart jumped down lightly and went towards them.

"And where was the digging party yesterday?" she demanded briskly.

The young man looked up and grinned.

"Shirley decided to go to town and shop. She took me, too. We didn't get home until after eleven last night."

The girl squatted back on her knees.

"You needn't put all the blame on me," she exclaimed indignantly, rubbing earth away from the plasterer's trowel she was holding in a strong brown hand. "If we hadn't relied on the local train being late, all would have been well. The train let us down. It ran on time."

" Personally, I'm all for trains running on time," said Miss Chart briskly. She bent down and inspected the ground that the girl had been working on. "Anything good? " she demanded.

The girl shook her head. " Not even a flint."

Miss Chart nodded her head towards Geraldine, who was standing in the background.

" I've brought a beginner to taste the delights of the dig. This is Geraldine Wilds. These youngsters are Mr. and Mrs. Rees—Geraint and Shirley. You might show Geraldine how to use a trowel, Shirley."

Geraldine was shown how to use the trowel. It was handled delicately, slicing neatly through the lump of earth that was being investigated. Each section was scrutinised carefully and slowly.

" If we found we were on to something good," explained Shirley, watching her pupil work, " we'd sieve every trowelful, just to make sure that there were no tiny pieces of bone or pot slipping past our eagle gaze. We've no reason to expect anything like that here, though, so just careful trowel work will do."

It was hot in the little hollow. The sun shone full on their faces, and Geraldine's shoulders began to ache with crouching in one position.

" Yes," said Shirley sympathetically, " it *is* hot. But then, our predecessors chose their sites rather cleverly, don't you think? You'll never find a camp like this one that isn't snugly tucked away from the wind and facing the sun. It must have been rather nice for the inhabitants, squatting outside their huts, chipping a bit of flint or working on a skin."

"It would have been nicer in the shade," submitted Geraldine.

"Might have been shade, in those days," said Shirley. "Easily could have been, because so much of the country was forest. Is scraping away with that trowel beginning to give you a crick in the neck? I thought it might. I suffered myself, when I was a beginner. Why don't you leave off scraping for a time and just scout around? It makes a change."

"Scout around?"

The older girl nodded.

"Prowl around with your eyes to the ground. It may not be authentic archæology, but it often brings good results."

So Geraldine relinquished the trowel and began to walk slowly round the hollow, studying each sprig of heather and each grey boulder very carefully. Miss Chart and Geraint were laughing together. Shirley joined them and began to help haul a bucket filled with soil from the hole that the others had dug. They were easy and care-free together. Geraldine, wandering about outside their immediate vicinity, wished she were one of them, and knew that she was not.

She could not help thinking that if Penny had come to the dig instead of herself, Penny would have been laughing and chatting as freely as the others.

"But it was kind of Aunt Pru to let me come," Geraldine told herself. "She knew I wouldn't be much help, but she did let me come."

Suddenly, something occurred to her. She smiled. Funny, she thought, but ever since that lecture I find it

quite easy to think of her as, and to call her, Aunt Pru.
I wonder if she has noticed? Penny was right. Aunt
Pru *is* nice!

And, looking from her own fair skin, that was beginning to redden with sunburn, to Miss Chart's brown face
under her greying hair, she even thought it would be
wonderful to look like that. Rather old, yes, but assured,
poised, certain of achievement.

Hot, aching, searching in the heather, Geraldine felt
very young, very much in need of a morale-booster.

She found it.

Lying at her feet, on a bare patch where the heather
branches did not spread, was a tiny arrowhead , a perfect
little thing that gleamed translucently. She bent and
picked it up, and there it was in her hands, with its tip
still sharp and two perfect little tangs jutting below it.

Miss Chart must have been watching her. " A find? "
she called.

Geraldine started to her feet. " This. It's lovely."

Miss Chart's voice stayed her.

" Don't move ! That's better. Have you marked the
place ? No ? Then mark it, before you move."

Geraldine took a round stone and a long twig and
made a marker for the place where the little arrow had
lain.

" Always mark such a place before leaving it," said
Miss Chart, advancing briskly. " It may seem easy to
remember, but, once you've moved, every bare patch
among the heather looks like the next one. What is it ?
Oh, I see. How very nice ! "

She turned the find in her brown hands.

" A perfect arrowhead," commented Geraint, in his soft Welsh voice. " It isn't often you come across one as perfect as this."

" Tangs and all," added Shirley, peering over his shoulder.

Miss Chart handed the arrowhead back to Geraldine. She smiled at her warmly. " Your first find," she remarked. " Are you excited about it ? I'm sure you are. We must let her keep it, mustn't we, Geraint ? As long as we have a record for the files about the dig, I think it would be all right for her to keep it."

Geraldine could hardly believe her good fortune.

" Isn't it valuable ? " she asked. " It looks as if it's made of some sort of precious stone. If it's valuable, perhaps it should go to a museum."

" That's flint," Miss Chart assured her. " It's fine and translucent, but still just flint. But your arrowhead is perfect. Often the tangs are broken or the tip blunted. Do you know how it would be fixed to its arrow ? See the tangs ? They'd be bound round and round with some sort of stout and springy stuff. Like as not, it would be catgut. It was an efficient little weapon in its day."

Geraint began to pace about the marker that Geraldine had made.

" It's rather a short distance from the camp itself. Myself, I'd say it came from an arrow shot by an attacker, that fell short."

" Could be," agreed Miss Chart. " The life of this little community might have ceased suddenly and with much bloodshed. It often did."

When this idea had been discussed, there was a pause

for a snack lunch, eaten lying in the springy heather, with fat bumblebees zooming near them. A buzzard wheeled slowly overhead, mewing in its queer, menacing way. Miss Chart lay on her back and eyed it speculatively.

" It's a big bird, nearly as big as an eagle, but I've seen a buzzard near Yr Hafan routed by a pair of magpies defending their nest."

" Have you many magpies at Yr Hafan ? " demanded Geraint, tossing a stone at a rabbit that had popped up and was regarding them from a safe distance.

The rabbit vanished.

" Several pairs," said Miss Chart. " They're handsome birds. They nest in the spinney opposite the house and help keep the pigeons away from the garden."

" My granny wouldn't have a magpie near her house," said Shirley lazily. " She says they're thieves."

Miss Chart laughed. " I don't know about magpies. I thought it was only jackdaws that had such a bad name. Well, we have jackdaws too, at Yr Hafan, but they mostly nest in the cliffs along with the seagulls and don't bother us."

When lunch was finished, work began again. Geraldine took her turn with the trowel, she helped raise buckets, she helped with a sieve, she grew more and more tired and sticky and hot. Even the other three were quieter, going about their tasks as a team, but not talking and laughing so much. The sun worked round to the west and shone redly over the distant sea. At last Miss Chart called a halt.

Shirley and Geraint set off together, swinging jauntily away over the hillside. " They've a tent in the valley below," said Miss Chart, " and not nearly so far to go as we have ourselves."

She led the way down the hillside.

" Well," she said after a silence, " now you know what a dig is like, and how boring it can be, and how little rewarding. Do you still want to be an archæologist ? "

" I think I do," said Geraldine, slowly and truthfully. " I think I do. I felt marvellous when I found the arrow-head."

Miss Chart smiled.

" Your first treasure, as mine is the little figure from Ur. Take care of it, won't you ? "

" Of course I'll take care of it," said Geraldine, and then added, because she had to make sure that she really was to keep it, " that is, if you are quite sure it's all right for me to have it."

" Quite all right," Miss Chart assured her, and began to lead the steep descent to the cottage. They reached the bottom at last, and stood, drooping with weariness, chatting to Jenny Jones before they got into the van.

It was sheer luxury to settle down into the padded leather seats and drive slowly home through the cool evening air. At the gate of Yr Hafan, Penny was waiting for them.

" Golly," she remarked, as the car drew up, " I thought you were never coming. I really did. And I've made a special supper for you because I thought you might be hungry. I was afraid you wouldn't be home to eat it before it spoiled. And lots of things have happened while you've both been away. There are letters from Mother and Daddy and another one from Auntie Clare.

And Dai's own special cow has had a calf, a heifer calf, and he seems pleased about it. Oh, and I nearly forgot. The seal has gone back to the sea. It went with its mother, on the afternoon tide. Dai and I watched it go. It swam quite well for such a baby."

She swung on Aunt Pru's arm as she chattered her way into the kitchen.

"Well, that's the best thing that could have happened to the seal," said Miss Chart.

"Gerry will miss it," said Penny.

"I won't," Geraldine assured her. "At least, not much. I've something else. Something that I found at the dig to-day. It's wrapped in my handkerchief. Here it is! See? What do you think of that?"

Penny inspected the arrowhead. "What is it?" she asked.

Geraldine touched it reverently.

"It came from an arrow. It's very, very old. It's the beginning of my museum."

She looked happy and excited, just as she used to look in Kenya.

Penny gave her a hug.

"I'm awfully glad you found it, Gerry. Find one for me, another time, will you? And now, do come and eat supper. I'm hungry myself, and it does smell rather good."

CHAPTER TWELVE

VANISHED TREASURE

"READY about!" called Dai.

The red sail flapped loosely above Geraldine's head, and then, as she remembered which rope she was to haul on, tightened. There came a subdued drumming in the rigging again, and the *Ibis* sped off on another tack.

Dai, sitting in the stern with one hand on the rudder, grinned at his crew.

"You did better that time," he said encouragingly.

"I did remember which rope"—began Geraldine, but he interrupted her.

"Sheet, not rope. We use ropes to tie up the cattle, not to sail boats."

"They look the same to me," returned Geraldine, with some spirit. She glanced down at the bulky yellow life-jacket she was wearing, and added, "Now that I know how to crew, do you think I could take this thing off? It's so very bulky and uncomfortable and rather wet."

"For one thing," replied Dai, "you don't yet know how to crew. Not by a long way. You're learning, but young Penny knows more about the *Ibis* than you do. It comes of wasting so much of your holiday sitting with your nose in a book, instead of in a boat. And for another thing, Miss Chart would never say ' yes ' to sailing without a life-jacket. She wears one herself when she sails."

"You're not wearing one," countered Geraldine.

"I can swim a mile," returned Dai. "I can, and that's not boasting. Even Miss Chart agreed that swimming a mile is the equal of a life-jacket."

"I can't swim at all," confessed Geraldine.

The boy sighed. "I suppose that means I shall have to take you in hand."

The calm water curled around the *Ibis's* prow, and Geraldine let one hand drift in it.

"You don't have to," she remarked.

"I like teaching you things," said Dai. His eyes, she thought, were as blue as the sea, and just for a moment it seemed as if she, and the *Ibis*, and Dai were all floating together in a dreamy wonderland. "And what are you doing with one hand in the water?" he asked. "Where will you be next time I call 'ready about'?"

"Ready for you!" retorted Geraldine.

They tacked to and fro and slowly brought the dinghy back into the haven. Penny, still clad in a wet bathing suit, ran out with the trolley and the boat was easily beached.

"You've been out an awfully long time," said Penny reproachfully.

"There's only a light wind," Dai told her. "We had to tack a lot to get out and in."

"If I'd come as well, you'd have had two in your crew," said Penny. "You'd have sailed better, because I know more about the *Ibis* than Gerry."

"Gerry's learning," Dai said. "She's a good pupil."

" She won't like you calling her ' Gerry '," said Penny.

Geraldine flushed. " I will. Why shouldn't I ? "

" I dunno," said Penny. " It was you who said you wouldn't."

Dai looked from one sister to the other.

" I'll stick to Geraldine if you'd rather I did," he said, " but, personally, I do think it's a mouthful. Besides, Gerry sounds more friendly."

" And anyway, we call you Dai," said Penny.

Geraldine looked surprised. " Isn't Dai your real name ? "

The boy laughed. " Indeed it is not. My full name is David. There must be some thousands of Davids in Wales, I should think. St. David's our patron saint, you see, and St. David's Day our national day. And Dai is short for David."

" But you pronounce it Die," objected Geraldine.

He nodded. " We do. It's the Welsh way."

Penny was tired of this discussion.

" The post came while I was swimming," she announced. " I saw the red van through the trees. I didn't go up to the house, because it isn't our day for letters from Mother and Daddy, and I didn't think there'd be any others for us. And the telephone van came as well, so perhaps the telephone has been repaired. I should think so anyway. The van soon drove away."

" You do keep an eye on what happens, don't you ? " asked Geraldine.

Penny was quite unperturbed. She merely said that it was nice to know what was going on, and by that time they had put the sails and the rudder tidily away in the boathouse. She slung her towel around her neck, and they started up the track to the house together.

"Come in for tea," urged Penny hospitably. "Aunt Pru is up at that dig again, but I know she'd tell us to have tea. If there isn't enough milk left afterwards, I'll walk up to the farm with you, Dai, and fetch some more."

Dai looked at Geraldine. "Will that be all right?" he asked.

It seemed silly to try to explain that her younger sister knew more about what was right at Yr Hafan than she did herself, so Geraldine nodded.

Penny led the way into the hall. Letters were lying in a small heap on the big chest; two of them were thin and blue. She darted forward with a squeal of delight.

"It isn't our mail day, but mail has come. Air-mail letters. They must be for us. Two of them. Here you are, Gerry."

"They might be for Aunt Pru," began Geraldine and stopped short. She suddenly realised that again she had called Miss Chart "Aunt Pru." She waited to see what her sister would say. But Penny was too excited to notice Geraldine's reference to Aunt Pru. She handed one letter to Geraldine and was now examining the other.

"This one says Miss Penelope Wilds, and that's me," she said. "I don't know about yours." Her voice trailed away as she tore the thin paper open. Her eyes opened wide, her mouth stayed open, too.

"Is anything wrong?" cried Gerry sharply.

"Wrong?" repeated Penny. "Wrong?" She smiled blissfully. "It couldn't be righter. Daddy's sold the farm. They're coming home. They're coming home soon ! "

" You're sure it's true ? " asked Geraldine. She fumbled with her own air-mail letter.

" Better read your own," advised Penny.

Geraldine read her own. She read how her parents would soon be back in England, how they hoped to find another, smaller farm in their own country and make a home together, again. It was wonderful, marvellous !

" So you'll be leaving us," said Dai, watching them read their letters.

" We only came for a holiday," said Penny.

Dai rubbed one foot on the floor.

" It's pleasant, here. I thought you might want to stay."

" Perhaps Aunt Pru will have us back another year," Penny said.

Dai waited, but Geraldine did not add to this.

" Where will you be living when your people come home ? " he asked at last.

" London, I suppose," Penny told him. " London, with Aunt Clare and Uncle Ted. We haven't anywhere else to go." She made a little face. " At least, I suppose we'll stay there if we can all fit in. Uncle Ted and Aunt Clare are most kind, but theirs is a very little house."

Still Geraldine did not say anything. She could not. She was simply bursting with mixed feelings. After missing her mother and father so terribly, failing to fit in at school, or with relatives, she was suddenly realising how happy she had been at Yr Hafan for the last few weeks. Ever since Miss Chart had first lectured her and then taken her to the dig. Since then, there had been so much to do. There had been the dig at Cader Mawr itself, there had been warm days on the beach with Penny, and there had been sailing and boating and swimming lessons with Dai. She was going to miss them all.

" You might stay here," suggested Dai slowly. " Perhaps your people could come here too. Yr Hafan isn't a small house. There's plenty of room in it."

Even Penny hesitated before replying ; then she said, " Aunt Pru isn't really our aunt, you know. She's Aunt Clare's aunt, and nothing to do with us except she's jolly nice. But I don't suppose she'd want Mother and Daddy as well as ourselves."

Geraldine made herself join in.

" It depends on what our parents want to do. Daddy writes that he means to buy another farm and start farming here."

" Here ? In Wales ? " said Dai eagerly.

Gerry saw that he was looking at her breathlessly, and felt a little breathless herself.

" He doesn't say Wales," she answered. " I imagine he's never thought of it. But—if he could find a farm near here—it would be wonderful."

" How about school ? " objected Penny. " We'd have to find another school, and I like the one I go to very much."

" There's a good school in our town," said Dai. " It isn't big, but we do pretty well. Every year somebody wins a scholarship. I shan't, but then, I'm not much of a scholar. I'll be lucky to get four passes next year, and then I'll leave and settle down to farming in earnest."

"Do boys and girls go to your school together?" asked Penny.

Dai nodded.

"We could go to school with you," said Penny thoughtfully. "That would be fun. How do we get there?"

"Walk two miles and then catch a bus," said Dai. "When it's raining, it's not as much fun as all that."

"What isn't as much fun?" demanded another voice, and they all jumped. Miss Chart was there, walking through the doorway.

"We've decided to call it a day as far as the dig goes," she announced, making for the chest and the remainder of the day's post. "Am I interrupting, by the way? Is this a serious conversation?"

"It's a beautiful conversation," Penny informed her enthusiastically. "We'd all come up from the beach and I was going to make tea, and then we saw there were these letters from home. And, only think, Aunt Pru! Daddy's sold the farm. He's sold it, and he's coming home quite soon. Daddy, and Mother too."

"Splendid for you," said Miss Chart.

"It isn't that we want to leave you," added Penny, feeling that she might have been too enthusiastic. "It isn't that at all. It's marvellous being here with you, but it will be wonderful to see Mother and Daddy again."

"Let's have that tea while we discuss it," suggested Miss Chart.

"I'll make it," said Penny, chattering happily. "I'll

make it, and if we're short of milk afterwards I'll go up to the farm and fetch more. I told Dai I'd do that. And, only think, Aunt Pru! Daddy's going to buy a farm here, and we think it ought to be a Welsh farm because Wales is quite wonderful and then we could go to school with Dai and he could finish teaching us to sail during the holidays." She paused on her way through the hall to the kitchen. "I think that would be heavenly," she finished quietly, before she ran on.

Miss Chart was watching Geraldine.

"And would you think that heavenly?" she asked.

"Yes," said Gerry, "yes, I would. But I'm not sure that good farms are to be found as easily as Penny thinks. And I don't know that Mother and Daddy would consider Wales. Perhaps they don't know Wales. I didn't, before we came here."

"And I gather that you now approve of it," said Miss Chart dryly. She turned towards her study, paused with a hand on the door. "I'll be along for tea in five minutes. Ask Penny to take out that plum cake, too, will you? I'm sure you're hungry, after sailing, and I haven't eaten since seven o'clock."

She vanished into her study, and Dai and Geraldine walked together down the hall.

Miss Chart followed them almost at once, and for the first time they saw her looking anything but calm and collected.

"Geraldine, Penny," she began, "have either of you moved the little gold figure that always stands on my study mantelpiece?"

Penny turned round, with the teapot in her hands.

" Why, Aunt Pru," she exclaimed, " we've been on the beach all morning ! "

" And sailing," added Geraldine. Then she realised what was wrong. " It hasn't gone, your special little statue, has it ? Not the first find, from Ur ? "

" It isn't on the mantelpiece," said Miss Chart flatly.

Geraldine found that she had crossed the big kitchen and was holding Miss Chart's hand.

" Don't worry," she said. " Please don't worry. It can't be lost. I'm sure it's just mislaid. Perhaps Dilys moved it when she dusted."

Miss Chart smiled grimly. " Dilys knows better than to move things from their places in my study." Geraldine thought she pressed her hand before she moved restlessly to the window. " Has anybody been up to the house this morning ? " she demanded.

" The post van, and the telephone van," said Penny. " I didn't notice anyone else, and I only saw those from the beach."

Miss Chart frowned. " Davies the Post and the Lewis Telephone are completely trustworthy. If the statue has been stolen, it was taken by an outsider. But only the statue seems to have gone. Why should a thief concentrate on that ? It's valuable, but there are other things more valuable in my room."

" Are you sure it's gone ? " asked Penny. She felt the question was perhaps superfluous, but Aunt Pru looked so miserable that she simply had to say something.

" Quite sure, Penny."

Aunt Pru walked out of the kitchen and Geraldine followed her. At the study door Miss Chart paused.

"Do you want to look to see if it's there? It's a waste of time. I'm quite sure it's gone."

Gerry stammered, "It's—just—I'm so awfully—sorry. I know how it feels. I know how I'd feel if I lost my arrowhead."

"I'll get over the loss," said Miss Chart.

Gerry drew a deep breath. "Would you like my arrowhead?" she asked. "If you would, I'd love to give it you. I know it isn't exactly the same as the little god from Ur, but it *is* my first find, and you can have it."

"Why, Gerry!" said Miss Chart. Her voice was soft and kind as it was when she talked to Penny. "Why, how very good of you! But no, I won't accept your arrowhead. It's valuable to you, you see, but not to me. It isn't *my* first find."

She closed the study door finally, but Geraldine did not feel that she had been shut out. She went back to the kitchen, fragrant with the smell of coffee brewing.

"I do like her," she was saying to herself. "Oh, I do. And I wish so much I could find the little statue. And she called me Gerry. I wonder did she ever notice that I called her Aunt Pru that first day we went to the dig?"

CHAPTER THIRTEEN

DANGEROUS VENTURE

A WEEK later Miss Chart drove Geraldine for the last time down the twisting lane that led from Jenny Jones's cottage. The dig at Cader Mawr was finished. Tools, and the few objects of interest that had been unearthed, were packed in the back of the red van.

"What are you thinking, Gerry?" asked Miss Chart suddenly. "That there isn't much to show for days of hard work?"

"That's true," admitted Geraldine, "though it wasn't what I was thinking. No. What I was remembering was Geraint explaining to me how the ancients lived, so long ago, in their little beehive huts. It couldn't have been as bad as all that. Shirley and Geraint told me how that long stone shelf built into the wall—you know, the one good wall we unearthed—they told me how a bed could be made on it with heather and bracken." She giggled. "Actually, we made a bed of heather on the ledge, and I tried it out. It was really very comfy, and Geraint said that if there'd only been a bear or a wolf or so, or other suitable animal for him to snare, I'd have had a fine coverlet. It might have been a bit smelly, though, don't you think?"

"I think you would very soon have found out how to

cure skins and so avoid the smell," returned Miss Chart. " Necessity is the mother of invention, you know. In fact, if everything had come easily to them, I doubt that our remote ancestors would have progressed at all."

" I think they had wooden doors to those niches in the walls that they used for storage," said Geraldine. " They could have done, if they were clever enough to work out how to build those huts. Geraint says there were forests everywhere, in those days, so there'd be plenty of wood. And wood would rot and leave no traces, so we have to guess."

" Guesswork," said Miss Chart reprovingly, " is not good archæology. Good archæology consists of making sure."

" Didn't you ever guess yourself ? Not even at first ? " Miss Chart laughed. She turned the van on to the wider lane and began to pick up speed.

" Of course I guess. We all guess. Very often a guess is all we have to go on—call it a hunch, if you like. But when we've finished guessing, we still have to make sure. And one thing I'm going away next month for, is to make sure of a guess of my own."

" I wish you weren't going," said Geraldine impulsively. " I know Mother and Daddy are coming home, and we'll all be together again, but I'll hate to think of Yr Hafan empty and lonely. I like to think of you living here."

" I like to live here myself," agreed Miss Chart. " After all, it has always been my home. My grandfather lived here, and my great-grandfather before him—he built the house. And my mother lived here after her marriage, because my father was a sea captain and it didn't matter where she made a home for him."

"So you grew up here?" asked Geraldine.

Miss Chart nodded. "I grew up here. I learned to sail in the bay and to know about farming. I went to school in our little town, the school that Dai Morgan goes to now. I used to ride there and back every day on a stout mountain pony. Nowadays, of course, you children are pampered, and are taken by bus."

"After we've walked two miles," said Geraldine swiftly. "I know, because Dai told me. I think I'd sooner ride the pony."

"But you wouldn't *mind* the two-mile walk? It would be twice a day, remember."

"I'd like it," said Geraldine. "I'm sure that I'd like it. There'd be so much to notice—birds, and wild animals, and the hills."

"And very often, the rain," added Miss Chart dryly.

"A good raincoat would take care of the rain," said Geraldine. She sighed. "Anyway, I shan't be walking to your school. I shall have to go back to the school in London, and travel by bus." She sighed even more deeply. "I'll have to make an effort when I do go back," she said. "I didn't like school very much when I started last term. I'll have to get used to it. And I *have* studied French, so I won't be as bad at that as I was."

"You've got a good brain," Miss Chart told her. "You shouldn't be really bad at anything, especially now that you seem to be growing up."

"Am I?" asked Geraldine meekly.

Miss Chart nodded. "Yes. Decidedly less adolescent

than when you first came here. I have hopes for you, yet."

She drove on, swung neatly past a large milk lorry that was taking up most of the road, and at last turned into the gates of Yr Hafan.

She looked at the stout stone house thoughtfully. " Actually," she confided, " I'm not sure that Yr Hafan will be left empty, this time when I'm away. I've heard of a couple who might be interested in taking care of it. If they are suitable, it would at least keep the house aired. Usually, I have to trust to Dilys to come in and light fires, whenever she thinks fit, and that, to put it at the least, is a great waste of coal and kindling."

Geraldine helped carry the tools into the shed, wipe them with oily rags, and store them away. Miss Chart carried the specimens into her study. She waved away the offer of further help.

" No. I shall catalogue these in my own way and write a short note about the dig. Apart from my own interest, I have to, you see. Nobody goes digging up sites in our countryside without convincing the Powers That Be that he's capable of doing a good job. You have to have a permit. After the permit, you have to show some results. So, you run down to the beach and see if Penny is swimming, while I settle down to my work."

Gerry ran up to her room, tugging off her sweater as she went. Dilys Owen was polishing the dark wooden stairs. " And is it Miss Chart back again ? " she asked. Dilys had now decided that Geraldine was not as bad as she had appeared on first acquaintance, and was quite friendly to her.

" Yes. We've finished the dig, and now she's writing it up," said Geraldine.

" A lot of nonsense, wasting so much time on things that are done with," grumbled Dilys. She began to rub the dark wood again. " And mind you how you go along the passage," she added to Geraldine, " I've only just finished that, and it's slippery."

Geraldine trod carefully and quietly along the passage, so quietly that she disturbed an intruder who was eyeing her dressing-table with interest. She drew up short in the doorway, exclaiming, and the intruder ran along the table hopped to the window sill, and took off from there with a flutter of black wings.

" What is it now ? " called Dilys.

" A bird," said Geraldine. " A biggish bird. It was on my dressing-table."

She ran to the window and peered out, and Dilys followed her, to look over her shoulder.

" A jackdaw, it is," said Dilys disgustedly. " Ones they are to make free of things. Look you now. Make sure this bird has not taken anything from your table."

Geraldine watched the bird fly into the distance, making for the cliffs that walled in the haven. She watched it flutter and settle on one of the cliffs.

" A nest it will have there, I doubt not," continued Dilys, also watching with her sharp brown eyes. " The times I have with jackdaws, especially when Miss Chart is away and we do not have regular fires in the hearths ! Nest in our chimneys, the birds will, and foul my hearths with the stuff they carry to make their nests. Still, I settled them, last spring. Tommy went up the ladder to the chimneys and fitted them over with wire netting, and that stopped the birds for the time. Now it looks as if they are nesting in the cliffs, along with the seagulls."

Geraldine withdrew her head from the window and inspected the top of the dressing-table.

" I don't think anything is missing," she said. " There wasn't much to take. And why should a bird want to take anything ? "

" Because," pronounced Dilys, " magpies and jack-daws, born thieves they are. Any bit of brightness that they can carry away, they'll take. Why, it was my own granny who lost her wedding ring, just after she had taken it off for the washing. Left it on the sill, she did, and a jackdaw came down and took it before she could do a thing. My granddad—he was a young man then—saw where the bird flew and followed it and climbed to the nest. He found the ring there all right, and a little cross that a neighbour had missed the year before."

" But a bird couldn't carry anything big," objected Geraldine. " It couldn't carry anything bigger than a ring, could it ? "

" I've heard of a jackdaw that stole a gold watch and chain," said Dilys, and went back to her polishing.

Geraldine stood at the window. She tried to make out just where the jackdaw had landed. It was, she thought, quite a broad ledge, and would not be too difficult to reach. She thought. She remembered Aunt Pru's little treasure from Ur that had disappeared so mysteriously over a week before. The little gold figure had been heavy, but small. It was not more than two inches high, and it shone brightly. If jackdaws loved bright things, she thought, one could certainly have glimpsed the little statue, hopped through the open window, and carried it away.

It was worth going to see.

She hesitated, wondering whether to tell Dai and Penny about her idea, but perhaps it would sound like a very foolish idea, if she explained it. Then, Dai might think she ought not to climb the cliff—it looked easy—but he might think not. The best thing to do was to run down to the haven and, if she had it all to herself, climb up and investigate the jackdaw's nest.

She was still wearing the old khaki shorts that Miss Chart had lent her, so the climb should be easy.

She raced down the path to the beach. Nobody was there, which surprised her, because she had expected Penny to be about, even if Dai were still at the farm. She studied the cliffs carefully, and realised that they were higher and steeper than she had thought. Still, there were plenty of hand and footholds jutting out, and the climb to the ledge where she could see an untidy tangle of twigs that must be a nest, seemed easy.

She walked across the sand to the tall rocks where the baby seal had been hidden. From the rocks, shingle led to stones that were interlaced with pools of water left behind by the tide. Geraldine picked her way carefully, climbing and twisting between the stones and, before she quite realised it, she was climbing higher, climbing the cliff.

It wasn't bad. She reached carefully for handhold after handhold, looked for a firm place to set a toe and, drew herself up. She did not look below her as she climbed, and the untidy nest jutting over the ledge came nearer and nearer.

A bird flew away from the cliff as she climbed, uttering a raucous cry of annoyance. Suddenly, the air near the cliff seemed full of birds, untidy black jackdaws, sleek grey seagulls, white terns, all annoyed and screaming.

A loose white feather drifted against Geraldine's face; she took no notice of it, but climbed on. At last she drew herself up on the ledge. It was narrow, far narrower than she had thought. There was just enough room for her to crouch there, with her hands free.

She peered into the nest. Her guess had been good, it was worth the climb. Shining in the middle of the litter that made it, was the little golden god from Ur. She picked it up gently and stuffed it into the pocket of her shorts. The nest was dry and fairly clean and empty, for the last brood that the jackdaws had reared there was fledged and had flown.

It was time to climb down the cliff.

For the first time, Geraldine looked below her. It was a long, long way down. The sea had risen and was near the rocks where the seal had lain. It was not the sea that frightened her, though. Suddenly, she felt sick. Her head swam. She shut her eyes and pressed hard back against the rock.

After a few minutes, she forced herself to open her eyes and look up.

She closed them again, shivering on the ledge in the hot sun.

There was no way up from her perch. The cliff overhung the place where she clung. She dared not look down because she knew that if she did, she would lose her balance and fall.

She did not know how long she crouched there, her sticky fingers clinging to the little gold figure in the pocket of her shorts, but, suddenly, from high above her head, a voice called, " Geraldine ! "

CHAPTER FOURTEEN

THE ANCHOR AND THE ROPE

DAI and Penny were late going down to the beach, as Mrs. Morgan, most unfairly, had insisted that all the week's collection of eggs should be washed before her son left the farm.

" Do it myself I would," she assured Dai, settling her best straw hat on her smooth hair, " but then, I'm going to town. Seldom it is I have the chance of going to town, so you must see the eggs washed and put ready for the egg van, Dai."

" And wait until it comes ? " asked her son dolefully. " Why, it may be hours. I may be here all morning waiting for it."

" No need to do that," said his mother briskly, picking up her purse and putting it in a capacious shopping basket, " Davies the Eggs knows where I leave my cartons, and he'll take them safely enough without you being there."

" Are there many eggs ? " asked Penny hopefully. She had counted on a sail with Dai while Geraldine was at the dig.

" A nice few," said Mrs. Morgan, with satisfaction. " The hens are laying well and there might be getting on for two hundred. Keep a count of them, Dai, won't you ? "

Dai groaned mournfully.

" Two hundred ! " he repeated. " Well, I thought there might be. The only thing is to get on with it and finish as soon as I can. I hope there's plenty of hot water in the tap."

" Plenty," he was assured. " But don't use it too hot. We don't want the eggs cooked inside their shells."

" Trust me to know that by now ! " returned Dai. He took off his jacket, rolled up his sleeves, and advanced towards the sink.

" I'll help with the eggs," offered Penny. " I don't mind if it means finishing quicker."

" It's a messy job," said Dai, taking a large brown egg from one of the bowls on the table and beginning to rub the shell clean. " Our hens *will* lay all over the place. I can't think why, when they've plenty of good, clean nests, but they do. There we are. That's the first one clean, anyway."

He stood the cleaned egg in one cup of a cardboard tray that was ready beside the bowls of eggs.

" Hens are contrary creatures," said Mrs. Morgan. She paused, on her way to the door. " Is there anything I can bring you back from town ? " she asked.

Dai grinned. " All sorts of things, but I've no money to pay for them."

" Right, then," returned his mother. " We'll let them wait until you have. And I shan't be back till milking time this evening, so help yourself to a meal out of the larder. There's cold boiled ham and cold chicken, so you won't starve."

She went out of the cool kitchen into the bright sunny

yard, and Dai and Penny heard his father's elderly car start up and drive away. It was very quiet as they worked side by side, cleaning eggs.

At last Penny drew a deep breath.

" I never knew there were so many eggs in the world before," she declared, " but you're doing the last one now and that's that. I don't think I'd like to be a farmer very much, if it means washing eggs every week."

" You have to take the rough with the smooth," said Dai philosophically. " On the whole, farming's a good life. I do believe that's a lorry coming down the lane. Look and see who it is, Penny. If it's the egg man, we're in luck. I'd sooner see these eggs stowed safely away than leave them to be picked up, whatever Mother said. I think she only told me to leave them so's not to spoil our morning."

Penny poked her head out of the door and saw the light lorry painted with the words EGG PACKING STATION on its side, backing into the farmyard.

" Good," said Dai. " Now we'll soon be off."

He carried out the cardboard cartons and saw them packed in the truck. He and the driver checked numbers and the driver signed a receipt. The truck drove away down the lane, and at last Dai was free. He shut the farmhouse door behind him.

" What shall we do ? " he asked. " Swim ? Or go out in the boat ? "

" Boat, please," said Penny promptly. She added, " Let's sail, too. Since Gerry started coming in the *Ibis*, I haven't done much sailing."

Dai flushed a little.

"Righto," he agreed hastily, "we'll sail."

They raced down the track towards the beach together and, as they passed Yr Hafan, Dai spoke hopefully.

"The van's back," he said, "perhaps Gerry will come out with us."

"She's probably helping Aunt Pru with the finds from the dig," said Penny disapprovingly.

They came out on the beach ; Geraldine was nowhere in sight.

"That's all right," said her sister. "She isn't here. She must be still with Aunt Pru, as I told you she'd be. Gosh, we're lucky ! The tide's just right, isn't it ? And there's a nice little wind. We ought to have a lovely sail." She gave her companion's arm an impatient tug. "Come along," she urged him. "What are you staring at ? "

"It's the birds," said Dai slowly. "Whatever has come over the birds ? They're behaving as if somebody was robbing their nests."

Penny gave a sudden small shriek and covered her face with her hands.

"Someone is," she gasped. "Someone is up there. Ever so high up. I can't look. It makes me dizzy to think of it."

"On the cliff——" began Dai. His words ended in a gasp. "It's Gerry ! " he added, in a breathless whisper.

Penny peeped through her covering hands and gave another shriek. Dai clapped a hard hand over her mouth.

"Don't make that sort of noise. Sound travels. Gerry looks frightened enough already. You don't want to make it worse, do you ? "

" But . . . if she falls down . . ." faltered Penny, taking her hands from her white face and staring at the forbidding cliffs, " if she falls down . . . she'll be killed."

" She won't fall down," said Dai. He seemed to grow taller as he spoke. " She won't fall down. We're going to fetch her up." He turned to the boat shed. " Run as fast as you can to Yr Hafan," he told Penny. " Get Tommy Owen, unless there's someone more able-bodied there. Be quick ! I'm going to take the boat anchor and the hawser to the top of the cliffs and try to bring Gerry up. There's six fathoms of rope on that anchor, and it's good rope and will hold. Don't panic, Penny. Get help. Get Tommy. Somebody. Anybody. And be quick ! "

Almost before Penny had regained the track to the house, he was following her with the anchor and its coil of stout rope in his arms. He turned away from the track and cut through bracken and heather towards the top of the cliffs. He said nothing as he went, conserving his breath.

He reached the short grass on the cliff top, threw down his burden, judged where Geraldine must be marooned on the ledge of the cliff, lay down on his stomach, and peered over the edge. The edge overhung slightly, but he could make out a bent leg some ten feet below.

" Geraldine," he called. No answer.

" Gerry ! " he called again.

Geraldine heard his voice, but she could not answer. All she could do was press desperately against the rough surface of the cliff, keep her eyes closed, and try not to hear the pounding of her heart and the roaring in her ears.

" Gerry," called Dai firmly, " I know you can hear me. You're safe, now. I've a stout rope and I shall make it fast and fix a noose in the end that I'll drop down to you. Pull that loop over your shoulders and under your arms and I'll help you up to the top. Just stay where you are. Don't panic. Everything's going to be all right."

He wriggled back from the edge of the cliff, grabbed the anchor, and looked around for a hold. There were no trees for miles around, but there was a high, worn stone. He twisted the rope round the stone and wedged the anchor at the back of it, driving one fluke into the stony ground as deep as he could.

Then he fastened a running noose at the other end of the hawser, working as carefully and slowly as he could bring himself to do. The noose had to run easily, and at the same time it had to hold tight.

When he was satisfied, he paid out what length of rope he thought would reach the ledge, took off his coat and laid it across the lip of the cliff, so that the hawser would not chafe, and then, with the noose in his hands, crawled to the edge again.

Geraldine was still there.

He made his voice cheerful.

" Noose is coming down, Gerry. It's safe, and the rope is strong. It will hold the boat in a storm, so you can be sure it will hold you. I'm going to drop the noose and when I see that you can reach it, I'm going back, to pull on the rope and help you climb to the top. Do you understand, Gerry ? "

He heard, straining his ears, a distant whisper. " I can't do it. I daren't let go. I daren't open my eyes."

" Keep your eyes shut, then," said Dai. " You'll be bumped and scratched a bit on the way up, but that won't matter. Just get the loop under your arms. Once you've done that, you're safe. Even if you don't try to climb, you'll be safe, because I've got the rope wedged, and I'll pull you up."

Another thin whisper: " I'll try."

" Rope coming down, then," said Dai, trying to be as matter-of-fact as if they were anchoring the boat. " Don't put on the noose until I whistle. There. That's good. It's touching you. Now, I'm going back to get hold of the rope. When I whistle, pull the noose over your shoulders and under your arms, and then you'll feel me start to pull."

He went back to the high stone and the anchor. They seemed firm. He bent, with his back to the cliffs and laid the rope across his shoulder. He whistled. The rope remained slack. He whistled again. This time it tightened across his shoulder.

He began to strain at the rope, using his strong young muscles as he had learned to use them about the farm, heaving sacks and churns.

He could hear a distant fall of stones and a scratching and slipping. The hemp cut into his shoulder with a fiery pain. Then feet rushed past his bent head, and he heard Tommy Owen's voice.

" Gently, now, girl. Gently, now. Here you come. Let me lie down and give you a hand over the edge. Hold my feet, Penny, while I lie flat. The girl will have to swing clear of the cliff before we can land her."

Dai strained at the rope. He wasn't sure, but he had a

terrified feeling that the anchor had shifted under the strain.

" Go on pulling," panted old Tommy, face down on the turf. " I've got the girl's hands. Keep the rope taut, or we'll both be over."

Dai kept the rope taut.

Other feet rushed by him, there was a sudden lifting of the strain.

" We've got her," said Miss Chart's voice. " Stop pulling, Dai. She's safe."

Dai fell over on to his side. He was too exhausted to stand up. His eyes were misty with sweat and straining, but he rubbed them clear and saw that Geraldine was sitting on the grass away from the edge of the cliff, and that Penny was holding her tight in her arms and they were both crying. Tommy Owen was sitting, too, his head resting on his arms, because he was an old man and had run very fast and had borne much of the strain. Miss Chart was standing, her face white.

" What nonsense is this ? " she demanded, in a clipped voice.

Dai did not answer. He put a hand to the shoulder that the rope had rubbed, and his fingers came away red.

Miss Chart walked towards him. She pulled his shirt away from the flesh. His shoulder was marked with an angry red weal.

" I'll dress that for you as soon as we get home," she said, in a kinder voice. " It must be very painful."

Dai managed to speak. " It is," he said briefly.

Penny loosened her arms from her sister's waist and ran across the turf. She pressed her face to Dai's shoulder. " You saved her, Dai," she said, still crying.

Dai looked most embarrassed. " I'm pretty strong," he muttered, " and I remembered the anchor and the rope ; they seemed the only way."

" But why," demanded Miss Chart, " was Geraldine in a position where she needed saving ? "

She had no answer, because Geraldine was still speechless from her ordeal.

Miss Chart shrugged. " We can't stay here," she observed. " Come along. I don't suppose any of you feels much like walking, but the best thing to do is to get home. You start, Tommy, and take it slowly. Now you, Penny. Dai, you bring Geraldine. Get up, Gerry. Pull yourself together. Yes ! You must ! That's better. I'll follow and bring the anchor and hawser. The first one home had better tell Dilys that we want hot strong coffee, and plenty of it."

The tattered little procession went slowly down the steep track and back to Yr Hafan. Geraldine's hands and nails were torn. Her face was swollen and smeared. There was a great tear in her blazer.

The deep cut on Dai's shoulder burned like fire. His arms felt as though they had been pulled out of their sockets. " Why did you climb so high ? " he muttered to his companion, as they followed Tommy Owen and Penny.

" It was the jackdaw," Gerry whispered back.

He stared at her bent head.

" Gerry, you were never so foolish as to climb up there after a jackdaw's egg ? Didn't you know there wouldn't be eggs in the nest this time of year ? If you'd wanted an egg, I'd have got you one, next spring."

" It wasn't an egg," said Gerry slowly. She pushed a hand into the pocket of her shorts and it closed around something smooth and hard. She drew it out. " There was a jackdaw on my dressing-table earlier this morning," she went on, " and Dilys told me what thieves they are. And I wondered about this . . . about the little god from Ur that disappeared from Aunt Pru's study. I thought a jackdaw might have taken it. And it was in the nest. It was ! But I never realised the cliff would be so high to climb, and I never thought about getting back."

" You might have been badly hurt," said Dai slowly, looking at the golden image in Geraldine's hand.

" I wanted it for Aunt Pru," said the girl simply.

Miss Chart, her arms full of anchor and rope, came swinging along behind them as they stood.

" What did you want for me ? " she demanded. She had been terrified when she realised Geraldine's danger, and her voice had hardened with fright. Now it was controlled and casual as usual.

Geraldine held out the image.

" This," she said. " A jackdaw *had* stolen it, just as I thought it might. That's why I climbed the cliff, Aunt Pru. To see if this was there."

Miss Chart shifted her burden so that she could take the golden god. Her voice trembled as she stared at it.

" You shouldn't have risked so much, Gerry," she said. " It wasn't worth it."

Geraldine hung her head.

"I didn't stop to think. It just seemed something I could do for you."

Miss Prudence Chart put the relic into her own pocket. She began to walk on again beside the boy and girl.

"Nobody has ever done so much for me before, Gerry," she said quietly. "Thank you very much."

"It would have been all right if I hadn't looked down from the ledge and gone dizzy," added Geraldine. "I couldn't help it. I just went dizzy and couldn't stir."

"Dai stirred for you, fortunately," said Miss Chart. "I think, really, I owe Dai as much as I owe you. Don't look so embarrassed, Dai. Come along. That shoulder of yours must be burning like fire. Let's get back to the house and dress it. I've some stuff that will take the sting away in no time."

"I'll be glad to try it," was all that Dai said.

CHAPTER FIFTEEN

THE CARETAKERS ARRIVE

EIGHT days later, Penny saw the red post van draw-ing away from the house. She made a dash for the front door.

"It's about time we had mail from home," she said firmly, as she ran. "I just can't understand Mother and Daddy. We've only heard from them once since they wrote to say they'd sold the Kenya farm, and I do think it's about time we knew when they are coming home."

Geraldine followed her sister at a more leisurely pace.

"There's sure to be air-mail letters to-day," she said.

Penny rushed into the cool hall and stared at the oak chest with disgust.

"Well, there aren't," she declared, in a crestfallen voice. "Look for yourself. All the envelopes are plain white—not an air-mail one among them." She riffled through the little pile of letters that Davies Post had left on the chest. "Nothing for us at all," she added, "not even a letter from Auntie Clare."

Miss Chart suddenly appeared at the door of her study.

"Was that the post?" she inquired. "I thought I heard the van, but I was too busy to go to the door."

Penny handed over the pile of letters.

" They're all for you," she said, sounding despondent. " I'm beginning to think Mother and Daddy have forgotten all about us. Or, perhaps Davies Post has overlooked all the air-mail letters."

" Your parents probably have a lot to do, now that they're leaving Kenya," said Miss Chart. She looked through her own envelopes and laid them aside. " Bills," she remarked, " and official stuff. They can wait." She inspected her visitors thoughtfully, and changed the subject. " It has seemed to me," she went on, " for some days now, that your heads have reached the stage when something must be done about your hair. Gerry's is shaggy, and Penny's is wild. I have to meet a train in town to-morrow morning. Would both of you like to call at the hairdresser's and have something done to your hair ? "

Penny groaned.

" I never heard of such an awful waste of a morning," she declared.

Even Geraldine was not enthusiastic.

" If we let it go a little longer," she said diplomatically, " there might be a rainy day. Having hair cut on a rainy day wouldn't seem so bad as having it done while the sun was shining."

" Only I might not be going into town," said Miss Chart. She waited.

Gerry sighed.

" Oh, well, if you think so, Aunt Pru, I suppose it really must want doing. And perhaps it won't take so very long."

" Hair can be a nuisance," agreed Aunt Pru sympathetically, " especially if it's supposed to be cut short. That's why I let mine grow and twist it into a bun. It's tidy that way, and stays put. I used to wear it bobbed, as you do, but there came a time when I was miles from civilisation for months. I only had a small mirror and I couldn't see much in that, so I just cut a chunk off my hair whenever it got in the way." She paused, smiling to herself. " I am not a vain woman," she finished, " but when I caught sight of the effect in a hotel mirror, I swore that it should never happen again. I don't aim to be glamorous, but it is pleasant to be tidy, and comfortable."

" I don't seem to have had time to look in my mirror very much lately," said Geraldine.

Penny inspected her sister thoughtfully.

" Now I come to look at you," she observed, " you do look a bit wild. Not that it matters, because we're on vacation, and there's nobody to look at us except Dai. I'm sure I look much worse than you do, because my hair always was a nuisance. As soon as I'm old enough, I'll let it grow and twist it into a bun, like Aunt Pru."

" Well, that's settled," said Aunt Pru cheerfully, turning back towards her study. " You might phone and make an appointment for two haircuts, will you ? The hairdresser is called Davies, H. G., and she's in the phone book. Make your appointment before ten o'clock, will you ? I want to be at the station by eleven."

" If you're meeting somebody at the station," Penny pointed out, " are you sure there'll be room for us in the car ? "

" I'll tell Tommy to put up the rear seat," said Miss

Chart. " It folds down to the floor and I hardly ever use it, but if he puts it up, the car will carry five with no trouble at all."

She went back to her study and the girls walked out into the sunshine.

" I wonder who's being met at the station to-morrow," said Penny. " Aunt Pru never said."

" It must be the caretaker people she mentioned ages ago," suggested Geraldine. " Don't you remember ? She told us she hoped to arrange for people to live here and look after Yr Hafan for the year she'll be away."

Penny sighed.

" I wish she wasn't going to leave Yr Hafan. When I'm back at school, I'd like to remember it like this, with Aunt Pru coming and going, and taking the boat out to the lobster pot, all just as it is now. Besides, if these caretaker people settle in, there may not be a chance for us to come back next August. There isn't much chance of that now, but I did hope, if I introduced the subject carefully, that Aunt Pru might agree to our coming back if Dilys would take charge of us."

" You're forgetting that Mother and Daddy will be here next year," said Geraldine.

Penny shook her head.

" No, I'm not. But we'll have settled down with Mother and Daddy again by next August, and it might be nice to have another holiday."

" I wonder where we *will* settle," said Geraldine, but there was no answer to that.

At nine o'clock the next morning, the red van was

waiting outside the front door. Penny opened the back and inspected it. Half the storage space was occupied by a bench seat which, when she bounced on it, proved comfortable.

"We shan't have much room to carry anything," she observed, craning over the back of the seat. "Aren't you doing much shopping to-day, Aunt Pru?"

Aunt Pru's shopping expeditions were remarkable for the size and the variety of things brought back from them. Often there were sacks and cases; once there had been a small calf that nibbled Penny's hair.

"I only expect these people to bring a couple of suit-cases," said Aunt Pru, getting behind the wheel. "I have been in touch with them about acting as caretakers for me while I'm away, and they're coming to look Yr Hafan over. I don't know whether they'll like the idea of spending the winter at Yr Hafan, not to mention next spring and summer. It is lonely in the winter."

"I'd spend any part of the year there, and it would be lovely," said Penny mournfully. So far, all hints as to a future holiday at Yr Hafan had fallen on surprisingly deaf ears.

"Are these people your caretakers, and are they staying the night, Aunt Pru?" asked Geraldine. She did not talk so much about leaving Yr Hafan as Penny did, but she felt about it even more keenly. In the few weeks they had spent there, the old house by the sea had become home just as much as the farm in Kenya had been home.

Miss Chart started the red van and drove away.

"To-night, certainly," she said. "Dilys has prepared

the room next to your own for them. If they like the idea, and if we like them, there is no reason why they shouldn't stay much longer."

" Haven't you met them before ? " inquired Penny, craning her neck to see out of the windshield, because the back of the car by her seat had no windows.

Miss Chart shook her head.

" They're strangers, but from what I've heard about them, I think we should get on very well."

They came to the little grey town that straggled alongside the river. There was only one row of shops, and Aunt Pru parked the red van under the trees that grew opposite them. She set off for her bank and to pay bills, while the girls made for the little hairdresser salon. There, gazing at herself in an unflatteringly large and well-lit mirror, Geraldine was forced to agree that it was certainly time her hair was trimmed. Even Penny was surprised at her looks. She sat in a chair and played with her hair while Geraldine's was trimmed ; when her turn came she had plaited the straggly growths into two thin pigtails and tied them together on top of her head.

" I think I'll stay like this," she said, staring at the result with fascination.

Geraldine stared, too, with horror.

" You can't, Penny. You look like something out of the zoo."

" I like to be unusual," stated Penny.

The hairdresser took charge competently. She swathed her younger customer in a flowery overall and began to snip.

"Your hair isn't as pretty as the other young lady's," she said, shatteringly and truthfully, "but there's no reason why it shouldn't be tidy. And if you took some trouble with it, you could coax a natural wave over your forehead. That's what you ought to do."

"Perhaps I will do that when I'm older," said Penny, watching her shorn locks drift to the floor. "Just at present, I haven't the time."

Both heads were trimmed, the hairdresser paid, and the girls wandered out into the sunshine. Across the road, a man was wading in the shining river, a long salmon rod in his hand. Beyond the fisherman they could see the high arch of the bridge that spanned the river, and beyond that, a jumble of grey roofs.

"That must be the school," said Penny, nodding her head towards the roofs. "Dai said it was beyond the bridge. It looks nice, doesn't it? Old. Friendly. Not like a school at all."

"Not like our school in London," agreed Geraldine. Her voice was very quiet.

Penny looked at her sharply. It crossed her mind that, now Gerry had settled down so happily at Yr Hafan, she might be as unsettled and sullen as ever when they returned to London, school, and Uncle Ted's house.

"Cheer up," she advised, "we're not going back just yet."

"Thank goodness!" added Geraldine, in a most heartfelt tone.

Miss Chart came out of the council offices, the rural equivalent of a Town Hall, and waved to them. They all climbed back into the red van and she looked at her watch.

" Ten to eleven," she said, " that's just right. We shouldn't have long to wait."

" As long as the train runs on time," said Penny.

" This one usually does. It's the main train of the day."

The car was parked on the sunny cobbles outside the little station, and the driver got out.

" Aren't you both coming too ? " she asked, one hand on the door.

Geraldine hesitated. " We don't know these people. Wouldn't we be in the way ? "

" You'd better come," said Miss Chart decidedly. " Remember, I don't know them either. Three pairs of eyes may be better than one pair, when it comes to spotting them."

" How shall you do it ? " asked Penny, with interest. " Are they going to wear something special ? Roses, or something like that ? And how will they know it's you ? They won't know what you look like, either."

" There aren't usually many people waiting on the platform," said Miss Chart. They all walked past the porter on duty. " Shall we have long to wait, Evan ? "

" Train's running on time to-day," returned the porter. " Look, the signal is up and there's the engine, just coming under the bridge."

Penny stared down the line.

" There are people with their heads out of one window," she announced.

Miss Chart was lighting a cigarette. " I wonder if

they're my caretakers," she said. The train came slowly, slowly, closer.

"It's Daddy!" cried Geraldine, suddenly and breath-lessly. "I know it can't be, but it *is* Daddy!"

Penny gave a squeal of delight and began to dash along the platform.

"It's Mother! It's Mother and Daddy! Aunt Pru, it's Mother and Daddy! Isn't it unbelievable? Isn't it marvellous? Oh, why doesn't the train stop!"

Bumping together gently, the four carriages of the little train drew up at the platform. Two people almost fell out of one carriage, and two girls almost knocked them over as they dashed forward to greet and hug them.

"You're taller," said Mr. Wilds to Penny.

"You're browner," said his wife to Geraldine.

Then they hugged one another again.

"You're just the same," said Penny, "just, just the same. Not taller or browner or older, but just the won-derful same."

Then Geraldine remembered something. She looked along the platform, but only two passengers had left the train. She turned around for Aunt Pru, but Miss Chart had vanished.

Geraldine suddenly realised something so marvellous that she could hardly believe it could be true. She had to make sure at once.

"Are you the caretakers?" she asked her parents.

Mother laughed. "We hope we are. Didn't you know?"

"Oh, no!" cried Penny. "It couldn't be! You couldn't be the caretakers."

Mother put her arm around her shoulders and began to walk towards the exit.

" Don't you want it to be true ? " she asked.

" *Want* it ? " repeated Penny. " It would be the most wonderful thing in the world. Ask Gerry. She feels like that, too."

" We felt it was an excellent idea, when Clare's aunt wrote and suggested this to us," explained Daddy, picking up a suitcase in either hand. " It gives us time to look round, time to settle down, to look for a place of our own."

" In Wales," said Gerry quickly.

Her father smiled. " In Wales, if we like it as much as you seem to do."

" You will," prophesied Penny. " I know you will. Only, it mustn't be too far away. We ought to settle here, near our friends."

" We have a year to make up our minds," said Daddy.

Miss Chart was sitting in the van, smoking furiously.

" Put the cases behind the back seat," she directed, obviously very much afraid of being thanked. " There isn't much room with the seat up, but I think we can manage. So Penny identified you without a rose or other marker ? That really shows you are learning to use your eyes, Penny."

Penny was not put off. She leaned behind the driving wheel and managed to give the aunt-who-was-not-really-an-aunt a giant hug. " You never thought of anything more heavenly," she said.

Miss Chart came up from the hug. She regarded Penny solemnly. " We don't know that they'll be willing to stay here and caretake," she said, in a conspiratorial whisper.

" *I* know," was all that Penny said.

They drove away from the station and over the humpy bridge. Gerry looked at the ancient buildings to the right—the place where Aunt Pru had gone to school, where Dai went, and where she and Penny might go. She did not speak much, because she was too happy, sitting beside her mother on the rear seat, holding her hand.

Squashed between her father and Miss Chart, Penny was chattering gaily.

" There's the shop where we had our hair cut . . . there's the ice cream shop . . . that's the school. Here's where we turn for the haven. Oh, you'll love the haven, Daddy. Can you swim ? I can, now. Dai taught me. Can you sail ? Dai is teaching me to sail the boat."

Father laughed.

" It sounds delectable and delightful, but how about farming ? Remember, I have a living to earn."

" Well, I expect Dai could help you about that, too," said Penny thoughtfully. " He wouldn't want to sell you his farm, because it belongs to his father and he likes it, but there must be lots of other farms and he'll know all about them." She bounced in her seat. " Now we're coming to where you get the first view of the sea. Watch for it ! There you are ! What do you think of that ? "

" I think," said Father quietly, " that Yr Hafan must be beautiful."

" I think it is beautiful," said Aunt Pru. " It's just a small grey house by the sea, but to me it's the most beautiful place in the world. I hope you will love it, too."

" I think we shall," said Mr. Wilds.

" You will," said Penny happily.

" You will," said Gerry. " I know you will."

And so, a united family again, they drove slowly down the steep lane and turned in at the gates of Yr Hafan— the Haven.